Vernon Robinson was born in London but raised in Lancashire. He was educated in various distinguished libraries. The author has worked at Manchester Daily Mail, Cambridge University Press and Unesco. He is a 4th Dan in Judo. He has an extensive library of Oriental and Western art and a large collection of Japanese Netsuke.

THE LADY FROM
MAIDA VALE

For Avril and Armande

Vernon Robinson

THE LADY FROM MAIDA VALE

AUSTIN MACAULEY
PUBLISHERS LTD.

A CIP catalogue record for this title is available from the British Library.

ISBN 978 184963 655 1

www.austinmacauley.com

First Published (2014)
Austin Macauley Publishers Ltd.
25 Canada Square
Canary Wharf
London
E14 5LB

Printed and bound in Great Britain

Acknowledgments

The author wishes to acknowledge a debt of thanks to the following: The National Gallery (London), Tate Britain, Mauritshaus (Amsterdam), and the Musee d'Orsay (Paris).

Prologue

Sleeping with the Enemy

Negresco Hotel, Nice, Cote D'Azur, France

From where I was sitting, I could see the young woman on the other side of the salon, just inside the entrance of this monument to the *belle époque*. She was the sort of woman one could not help but notice. She sat with her legs crossed in an ornate, high-backed chair, slightly to the side (presumably because she could look at the entrance). She wore a Dior yellow silk dress that flowed over her tall slender figure like a stream. The dress was buttoned over her bosom, and gathered at the waist by a white belt fastened by a complicated gold clasp in the shape of a snake. Her hair was blonde (naturally so); it was worn neatly short, and the ends curled under the lobes of her ears. She wore a fine gold chain round her throat with a pearl in its centre. Her hands were folded in her lap and held a pair of Chanel sunglasses. She wore a gold Cartier watch on her right wrist. I saw her uncross and cross her lightly tanned legs: on her feet she wore high-heeled Jimmy Choo white sandals.

Actually, I was looking into a long mirror on the other side of the salon, and the person I was looking at was me; and, not for the first time, I thought, *You are everything an excellent mistress should be: beautiful, elegant, discreet, worldly*; so I was waiting for a gentleman, a gentleman whom I knew very well, meeting in this awful, overblown, expensive hotel.

And here he was.

Carlo Palladio, entrepreneur, billionaire businessman, patron of the artistic and social elite of Milan – scion of a family that could trace its genealogy to the de Medicis. I looked over my shoulder as I heard the roar of a powerful automobile along the Promenade des Anglais – it stopped outside the cupola of the Hotel Negresco where the Promenade joins the rather scruffy side street.

Carlo strode in, looking round, then he spotted me. "Dawn!" He slid into the chair next to mine, bent over, kissed me on both cheeks, then lifted my hand and kissed that as well. I was amused, always, at his extravagant gestures. He said:

"You came! *Bella come sempre*"

"Of course – don't I always?"

He was dressed in a navy-blue blazer with gold buttons, cream chinos, a white shirt with a red silk cravat; on his feet, highly polished loafers. Carlo Palladio was 48 years old, medium height, tanned, broad shouldered. He kept his figure by swimming ten lengths in the pool at his villa outside Milan every morning. Our meetings were always arranged by Carlo. I would collect a first-class ticket at Heathrow and come straight to the Negresco. But he didn't treat me like a tart. He was always polite, respectful, and courteous. I loved him, and he me; I also liked and respected him.

He was married of course. I had once seen Signora Palladio from a distance: a tall, beak-nosed *grande dame*. She was devout and on the board of trustees of the Duomo. Whether she knew of our meetings – well, she could probably guess. No doubt she would shrug her shoulders ('Italian men…'). The important thing was that Carlo should not bring the family into disrepute (they had two sons and a daughter), and threaten their position in society. That would be unforgivable.

A pause. For at that moment I recalled a paperback I found in the JCR at London University. A surprising find in the sociology department, for it was a guide to being a whore–

1. Always be in control of the situation. If you have any doubt about the client or his intentions, walk away. Trust your instincts.

2. Always choose men of forty years or over and who are patently rich: they feel they have nothing to prove. All they want is the company of a beautiful woman who complements the idea they have of themselves.

3. Always be impeccably dressed and clean: first impressions are vital. Men I have described have certain expectations; do not disillusion them.

4. Never wear 'tarty' underwear. The type of client you are hoping to attract will think you look cheap – which you are not. Red and black knickers and lacy stockings are for page 3 girls. Always wear silk and lace in pastel colours.

5. Always try to make intelligent conversation, and show a keen interest in him and his business and leisure activities. Fluency in a language other than English is always an added attraction.

All the above will ensure that you attract the best clients and therefore earn the most money. Once learnt, it is a simple process. Men are easily guided. Oh, and always take the money first.

(Feeling rather naughty, I had pinched the handbook. Perhaps one of the female students was considering taking whoring as a job – it seemed appropriate, somehow, for a sociologist. Just think, she could have done a PhD on it!)

"Tell me, Carlo: you are well?"

He waved a hand. "I am with you. It is a beautiful day. My businesses are a concern at times… but we forget that!"

I couldn't imagine Carlo losing sleep over it, even with all the fingers he had in many pies – property, shipping, fashion houses. We had lunch on the terrace overlooking the Promenade des Anglais. In front of the terrace is a balcony filled with plants and flowers. We ate lobster salad and drank a carafe of rose, looking over the sea: it was getting hot, the sun striking the Mediterranean like a white bolt. We sat silently for a while, finishing the wine; then I put my hand over his and said: "Siesta."

He followed me silently. In the lift to our suite, I held him and he kissed me on the throat.

I woke before Carlo: he was still sleeping like a babe (as well he should). I looked round our room. This again was a monument to 19th century decadence: fantastic satin drapes across the tall windows, chairs in the style of Louis XV, with ornate gold edging, and silk cushions and coverlet on our enormous bed. I looked across at an ormolu mirror: I felt like Madame de Pompadour (only the French would turn a hotel devoted to decadence into a National Monument). I slipped out of bed wearing nothing but my silk kimono.

That evening we would be dining by the harbour in a small bistro, so I laid out his casual clothes and mine. Carlo stirred, opened his eyes, and stretched. He blinked as if seeing me for the first time. I said:

"Come on, lazy bones; I'm running the bath."

We lay opposite each other, touching toes in the enormous marble bath.

Carlo said: "You are wearing red nail varnish on your toenails?"

I flicked suds at his chest. "You don't like it?"

"Yes, yes. Of course! I like all of you!"

"So you have demonstrated many times, my sweet."

He laughed out loud. "Dawn – you are unique! You are what the English call the cool client."

"Cool customer?"

We strolled down the rue Massenet, and turned towards the Promenade. The rest of the weekend passed like that: every evening we would stroll down the Promenade, arm in arm like an old married couple, and sit in a harbour-side restaurant, watching the sun go down over Antibes, after a day driving around at top speed in his Ferrari up to the perched villages – la Turbie, Sospel, Eze; the latter was the place Carlo liked the most – I suppose because of its spectacular position. Eze is more than 400 feet above sea level, and he drove his Ferrari round hair-pin bends at a ridiculous speed. All this, for Carlo, I suppose was him breaking out from his respectable position in the Milanese business community – freedom to act like the young blade he once was. He drove the red toys-for-the-big-boys car into the courtyard of the Manoir de la Chevre d'Or hotel. I thought, *Why would they name this splendid establishment after a goat? Even a golden goat?* Had it anything to do with the fact that only a goat could climb up these mountains? Or did it go back to pagan eras?

We left the Ferrari in the hotel's car park and strolled across the edge, leaning on the rail. Across the horizon – through the midday haze – we could see the coastline stretching into the far distance: Cagnes, Antibes... They say one can see Corsica on a fine day. I doubted it. Just below us was another small balcony. A crowd of chattering Japanese were eating a late lunch alfresco. We joined them for the hotel's speciality dish, 'four fish' with mashed potato, followed by citron tart. I drank white wine; Carlo, water (he might have been an overgrown schoolboy, but he wasn't a fool).

At this level, Eze's hotels and boutiques have been, literally, carved out of the rock; but Carlo and I walked away from them, through a long narrow street and climbed up to the botanic garden. Between the succulents were impressionistic sculptures about four feet high – female, of course – I took a photograph of Carlo with his arm around one.

We got back to the Negresco about five in the afternoon and lay on our bed; Carlo started to complain about the pain in his calves, so I dug my fingers into the muscles, massaging.

"Dawn, You are a cruel woman!"

"Lie still and don't be such a baby." Honestly, men...

He fell asleep as usual, but I was awake, thinking, looking at the ornate ceiling. As usual on our final evening together we always went to Monte Carlo; he fantasised about being named after the place. But I could not imagine my lover's family stooping to the idea that they had anything to do with such vulgarians as the Grimaldis. But Carlo liked to splash some money at the casino and show me off in the grill room at the Hotel d'Paris in the cupola overlooking the casino.

That evening I wore a purple (definitely that season's colour) Valentino dress. It was gathered at the waist and fastened at the side; the skirt flowed to my knees. Before we left the hotel, Carlo placed a slim red leather case in my hand; a gold inlay ran round the edge. I knew immediately who the maker was and what it contained. Carlo turned me round, and fastened the clasp round my neck. I ran to the mirror and watched the diamonds reflect in the glass like white fire. I gasped:

"Oh, Carlo –it is amazing!"

"*Ti piace*?"

I hugged and kissed him. "*Mi piace daveno!*"

"And also, Dawn, I have news for you – they want me to become a Euro-MP."

"I knew you were going to tell me something; I saw your photo in the *Corriere della Sera*. You were standing next to Berlusconi. I never knew you were interested in politics, Carlo." (I hope Carlo knew what he was doing, mixing with that aged roué with the dyed hair.) "Well, darling, I can only wish you well – but be careful of that man."

"*Grazie* – now! We go and have a wonderful evening."

Which, of course, we did. Looking back, a small detail remained in mind. I said to myself, after that 'light lunch' how would I face dinner? But we didn't eat until nine that evening; Carlo threw hundred euro notes around the casino like falling autumn leaves. He finished by losing just 500 euros; I won 100 out of a stake of 1000. 10% – not bad.

As I looked out of the window over Monaco at the Hotel d'Paris grill room, a curved line of coloured lights stretching into the distance – how many times had I stared at the end of an evening here!

I woke in the night. Carlo was sleeping like a baby, and I packed our baggage for the morning. I looked down at Carlo, his arm flung out of his side of the enormous bed, exposing his strong chest. *Carlo,* I thought, *you are quite a man – we have come a long way since we met in the Cipriani, Venice.*

But that was a long time ago…

***

I was recalling every detail of that assignation sitting in a taxi on the way to Nice airport, yet again. Nobody would have suspected that the days I had just spent with Carlo were any different from the others – a round of sunbathing, swimming, eating, and drinking. What Carlo didn't know was this time he was sleeping with the enemy. As we approached, the taxi swerved across the road by the roundabout (near that horrible enormous wire sculpture of a human figure). I paid him off and ignored the porters.

I had a first-class return ticket to London, but that was not my first destination. I got a refund on the ticket and crossed over to the Air Switzerland desk and booked a business class single Zurich-London for the next day, then made my way to the Ladies' loo. When I emerged, I was hopefully a different person. I had removed my make-up, changed into a dark-blue trouser suit; underneath that I wore a high-necked white collarless blouse (which hid the necklace). I wore black-rimmed plain glass spectacles.

I was now as anonymous as I could be. There is no point taking a taxi at Zurich airport: there is a regular bus shuttle to the city centre, which always runs on time with the usual deadly German-Swiss efficiency. I booked in at the usual small pension then walked down the Bahnhoffstrasse to my bank (dodging the trams as I crossed the road – the only time when I do not feel safe in this town).

They checked my palm print at the entrance to the vault, then a thin-lipped young man gave me my key. He left as I opened my safe deposit box. I placed 5000 euros of the 7000 Carlo had given me into the box and also the diamond necklace (after all, a girl has to look to her future, hasn't she?). I left the bank just as they were closing and made my way to the lakeside; it was now nearly the 'aperitif hour', so I reckoned I had earned a drink.

I was looking over the grey water and sipping a *kir royale*; I could just make out the towers at Bollingen, where Carl Jung used to take his lesbian mistress, Toni Wolff – there's a nice psychological conundrum for you! I heard his footsteps: it was the same young man from the bank. I said:

"Sit down, Franz."

He did as I asked, but nervously.

"Drink?"

"Thank you, but no, Fraulein Hope."

"I think our business is now conducted satisfactorily, don't you agree, Franz?"

He nodded, cleared his throat, and then said: "You know, of course, Fraulein Hope, that I would do nothing that would compromise the integrity of the bank."

I nearly laughed out loud. *Oh, no?* What about a spot of insider trading that had just netted us both 50,000 Swiss francs? These Germanic puritans would say anything that would clear their conscience, while forgetting at the same time that they had broken the law. (I said to myself, *You weren't like this when you thought you were going to be seduced. Sorry, Franz: but I was more interested in your father's dealings than going to bed with you.*)

"Of course not, Franz: you are a conscientious employee. By the way, how is your fiancée?"

He blushed. "We marry in six months' time."

I finished my drink. "Then you will find the money very useful, no doubt."

He stood, bowed stiffly, and then vanished.

After an excellent dinner and a sound, dreamless sleep I caught the first flight, Zurich-Heathrow. Business class was half empty; I'd had enough of haute cuisine, so I drank green tea and nibbled at wholemeal biscuits, stretching out on two seats and reading *The Prince* all the way to England.

Airports, airports... It was when I made my way to the Border Agency and passport control and joined the tiresome queue with increasing impatience that a voice behind me said:

"Dawn Hope?" I ignored the question; he knew who I was; after all, I had advised the Department of my ETA.

"Come on, Dawn."

I turned. The speaker was a broad-shouldered young man grinning at me. He put his hand into the inside pocket of the leather jacket, opened a small wallet and showed me. It was an identification card that held his photo, showing him to be Inspector John Hibbert of the Metropolitan Police – a Special Branch officer no less.

I said: "Hello, John. Have you been following me?"

"I don't have your expensive tastes. How was the Cote d'Azur?"

"The sun was shining. I suppose your boss is here."

"Of course. Do you have your ID? Then we can avoid this crowd." I showed it to him, plus my passport. But I didn't want any of my fellow Customs officers at the airport clocking me – or the Border Agency people who would make a great show of waving me through. Neither agency likes the other very much: Revenue and Customs considering the Border people too lax (read your newspaper). As we reached the door of a small office labelled H.M. REVENUE AND CUSTOMS, Hibbert said, "Glad to be home?"

I didn't answer. He followed me into the plain little room; there was a frosted glass window at the far end; in the middle a scratched wooden table; and two chairs opposite each other. One was occupied by a middle-aged man wearing a lightweight tweed suit, a check shirt, and a dark-green tie. He had a cardboard folder on the table in front of him.

"Good afternoon, Miss Hope. I'm sorry for the inconvenience: please sit down. I won't keep you long."

Why was he apologising? We were on schedule. But meet Commander Duncan Maddox, the old-fashioned gentleman-civil servant. Well, he might look like that, but don't be deceived; this guy was as ruthless as they came; he would throw you to the wolves and apologise at the same time.

I said: "Hallo, Commander: what can I do for you?'

He smiled thinly. We both knew the answer to that. He said: "Did you have a nice weekend, Miss Hope? Weather pleasant?"

"Yes to both questions." I passed the CD-ROM to him, wrapped in a plastic envelope.

Maddox slid it into the cardboard folder. He had further questions: "And what is your assessment of the situation apropos your friend Mr Palladio? Will he change direction? Expand his interests?"

"I should say so: he said quite plainly," (if an Italian says anything plainly), "that Berlusconi and he are close. But Carlo never does anything for nothing. I think we can assume that his motives in wishing to become an Italian MEP are far from altruistic. But I ask myself one question, Commander…"

Maddox sat up. "And what is that, Miss Hope?"

"Look: Carlo is no fool. Why does he want to do this? This is a man who has everything. I think this is payback time…"

"To whom?"

"You mean *for* whom – if we are going to be pedantic. That younger son of his, Aldo, is a bit wild. Carlo may worry what Aldo gets up or the company he keeps. But he has his own private snoopers. All the info on Aldo's movements are on the CD-ROM – downloaded by me when Carlo was asleep. And nothing to do with the crazy idea (who had it, by the way?) whether Aldo recovered the Raphael *Portrait of a Young Man* stolen by the Nazis during World War II for that fat slob Goering's private collection. I still believe that if Aldo found it and tried to do a deal with the Russians, which I doubt… Look – I'm tired – had a long day. Can I go now?"

Maddox stood. "The Department is most grateful…"

"I should bloody well hope so. My usual charges apply. And make sure Accounts pay before the end of the month, the skinflints."

Maddox held out his hand, which I didn't shake. I said: "And what about my luggage? And how do I get home, Commander? Any chance of a lift?"

He waved a hand. "I'm sure John will take care of you." I left, but didn't say goodbye to Maddox. Whether Hibbert liked being my escort and chauffeur, he didn't say; I had a feeling that John didn't really like me (as you will find out later) and he was quiet all the way through the sprawl out of Heathrow. By the time we reached what he usually called the 'posh end of Elgin Avenue' he had not said a word.

I thanked John as he passed me my baggage out of the dark blue Audi.

He smiled. "That's OK, Miss Hope, all part of the service. Would you like my help in unpacking? Run your bath? Scrub your back?"

"Very funny, Jeeves. Goodnight and thanks for the lift."

Chapter One

Maida Vale, London

Home, sweet home. It was as quiet as the grave. I entered the house I shared with my father and wandered in to his study at the right-hand side of the hallway. Empty. I called out to him: "Dad, I'm home." No answer. I walked into the sitting room. Empty. I had a sudden feeling of panic, rushed upstairs and knocked on his bedroom door. No answer. I opened the door. He was lying on the duvet, propped against the pillows: he had fallen asleep. I looked at the book that had slipped on to the carpet with his reading spectacles. It was one of his favourites – C. P. Snow's *The Affair* (no, not about a love *affaire* but a scandal in a Cambridge college concerning a scientist accused of plagiarism).

My apartments were on the floor above my father's; I had them decorated to my own taste since my mother died. If you thought that they would be all gold drapes and red wallpaper, you'd be wrong: I may be of doubtful morality (and I don't mean just sex), but I have excellent taste; and I am exceptionally well educated. More Laura Ashley/John Lewis than a whore's boudoir. The walls in my bedroom were pale green with a faint silver spring flower motif. My double bed had a cream duvet; three crisp white pillows lay against the leather headboard. On both sides of the bed were two cream Georgian style cabinets, one of which held paperbacks – mainly art-history and biography. On the wall above my head were two framed prints by Fragonard. When I looked across on to the wall at the foot of the bed I could see myself in a gold-rimmed, oval mirror.

The third floor (strictly, the attic) was fitted out as an office. I had a computer and a printer on the beech veneer desk. There was no landline phone: but two cell phones, one of which had a direct line to the Department. Bookcases lined the rear wall; they held everything, from undergraduate language texts to coffee table art books, to Inland Revenue and Home Office regulations. There was a pair of night-sight binoculars (whose case was stamped with the order, 'Property of H.M. Govt., do not remove'). Taped under the desk was a 9 mm Glock 26 automatic pistol.

This upper floor of the house was my refuge; no man had slept in my bed. I unpacked while running a bath; everything was put away neatly, my precious silk dresses covered with cloth bags and hung in the wardrobe; my laundry straight in the basket. As I lay in the scented warm water, I thought of Carlo Palladio: *You are quite a man, Carlo – and I have just betrayed you.*

I got out of the bath and stood under a cold shower, dried myself quickly and wandered about my bedroom naked, making wet footprints on the deep pile carpet. I halted and looked at myself in the long mirror, nude. *My goodness, Dawn, you do have a marvellous figure.* 'Goodness'? That was a laugh. I danced around the bedroom, running my hands through my hair, feeling as free as the wind (what would the prissy language mistress Miss Prescott at St Edmund's Academy think if she could see me now?). I found silk pyjamas and kimono in the second drawer of the Chinese cupboard in the second bedroom.

Downstairs, in the kitchen freezer, I found a Waitrose frozen fish dish and bunged it in the microwave, then opened a bottle of Sancerre. I sipped a glass of the white wine and wandered into the sitting-room while waiting for my meal to cook and looked out of the window. The clouds that had greeted me at Heathrow and seemed to follow me on the journey here had dispersed; it was now a clear blue evening.

I heard my father's stair lift move downstairs. It stopped, then his voice. "Dawn!" Leaning on his stick, he joined me. I went over and kissed him. I gave him my inspection – the one reserved for when I had been away. He looked good. I said:

"I hope that you've been looking after yourself, Dad."

He sat in his favourite chair. "Don't I look well? And I will have a glass of Sancerre, please."

"Have you eaten? Are you hungry? We could share…"

He shook his head. "Mrs Mills left me something." Mrs Mills was our 'daily'.

"And," I replied, "what have you been up to?" But I felt a certain stiffening in his attitude; I shouldn't have asked that. My father knew where I had been and with whom. His thoughts would be, *I am not allowed to ask your business – so why ask mine?* I suddenly felt a shock run through me – it would be dreadful if our relationship should be tarred by that attitude. When I looked at my father again, I saw that I might have misread his body language – he was chuckling, his body stirring with laughter. What was all that about? Eventually he said:

"Actually, daughter dearest – I haven't been here."

"I beg your pardon?"

He continued: "Well, the day after you left Anne and I went to the east coast for the weekend. The sea air did us both good, and we ate lots of fresh fish." My father was really feeling pleased with himself. (All right, I knew that he and Dr Anne Holt, the distinguished anthropologist, had been friends for more than a year – but I didn't know it had got that far. I was quite put out.)

"That was nice." It seemed a feeble remark.

He said, "I don't know whether you have noticed, Dawn – but do you think my mobility has improved?"

"Well, yes – I suppose I had." (Where was this coming from?)

He smiled again. "I've being having a course of acupuncture – a Chinese woman Anne knows. I was doubtful at first, but I now have confidence in Doctor Lee. I feel a definite improvement in my mobility."

All this information was difficult to absorb, so I made all the right noises and poured him another glass of Sancerre.

As I lay in my bed, tired after the day, I thought about what my father had said – the old devil! But where was their relationship going? But then I had a cold feeling about Carlo – all we had meant at our rendezvous. I felt rotten about what I had done – or what was about to be done to his family.

Buona notte, caro.

A new day and I awoke, stretched, and luxuriated in the warmth of my bed. I turned my head and looked at the day through the long net curtain: another clear, pale-blue sky. I felt lazy, even after an uninterrupted eight hours' sleep. *The trouble with you, Dawn, is that you have got used to too much dolce vita.* I threw back the bedclothes, wrapped a robe around me, and opened the bedroom window; a soft breeze moved the long net curtains and freshened the room. I washed, dressed, had a breakfast of muesli and toast and freshly ground coffee. I drank three cups while I tidied and sorted my laundry.

By ten-thirty, I was sprawled on the sofa, when my cell-phone rang (the one linked to the Department).

"Yes?"

"I would like to discuss the information you supplied."

"When?"

"About an hour? The usual place."

"Very well." I do wish he wouldn't play silly TV spook games. But what to wear for such an assignation? A military-style mac and a slouch fedora? *Perhaps not.* I smiled to myself as I divested myself of jeans and T-shirt and donned a cream linen dress and a scarlet belt. I drove my Mini Cooper into the car park at the Iveagh Bequest. Maddox was waiting outside Kenwood, sitting on a park bench, looking down the long slope that was the lawn extending from the house. There were young children with their mothers, who were watching the brood running up and down the hill, flying a kite. The multi-coloured shape swooped up and down in the breeze then clonked on to the grass as one of the children lost control.

I placed myself next to Maddox and waited for him to say something. The breeze dropped suddenly and the children got tired of the kite-flying, so ran off to their parents; I heard them demand food and drink. Maddox said:

"Shall we walk?"

We made our way to the house.

I slid my arm through his; he flinched, and I said, "Let's keep up the pretence, Commander, shall we? Do you have a shadow?"

"No, Miss Hope."

"OK: but I've only got your word for that, haven't I? Let me give you a tour of the paintings." I was being deliberately obstructive; but sod him. We stood in front of Vermeer's 'Girl Playing a Guitar'. I said; "Isn't that just exquisite? Look at the way the golden light from the window shines on her left shoulder and on the instrument. Do you realise how much it is worth?"

"I don't have your aesthetic leanings, Miss Hope."

"Don't be pompous. It is absolutely beautiful." This was always the price Maddox paid when I met him after an operation; for very often, it involved personal hazard or danger to me at the time – so he put up with it. (Talk about casting pearls before swine...) We reached the end of the tour; Rembrandt's painting of himself in old age; one of the most moving – and scary – pictures I had ever looked at. His whole life was in that expression – making the viewer realise that Rembrandt was reminding us all of the message, 'That was my life, what do you make of it? I was the greatest painter of my century. In the end, what did it do for me? Think on your life.' *Vanity, vanity. All is vanity...* But even though Rembrandt had frightening talent, he remained humble before God. *Quo Vadis*?

I didn't actually say that to Maddox, of course. We went outside and walked under the rose bower. I said: "Speak to me, Commander." Would I never get under his skin? Not him: he was the last of the stiff-upper-lip characters; duty was all. Did he have a wife? Children? But that was pointless speculation.

He said, "Would you care for a cup of tea?" We sat in the cafe; the only other customers were two elderly women, with their backs against the window, at the far side.

I said, "Well?"

Maddox replied briskly: "What you retrieved was some of Palladio's day-to-day business transactions. But the rest was in the form of a report of Aldo's movements and meetings over the previous months. Then there is a record of emails to Aldo, asking about his business dealings; warning him to be careful, because his father has his suspicions about the legality of said son's activities."

"Narcotics?"

Maddox shook his head. "The suspicion is that Aldo is smuggling *objets d'art* out of Italy. And you know how itchy the Italians are about that."

"Really – which sort? Bits from the Sistine Chapel ceiling? Or Bernini sculptures? Apart from anything else, they'd be one helluva weight."

Maddox ignored my sarcasm. "Have you heard about the so-called 'lost' Leonardo?"

"Of course. There's a professor at the Uffizi who has been searching for it for thirty years. The so-called experts think it's the fresco 'Battle of Anghiaria' (personally, I think it's a contemporary copy – if they ever find it somewhere in the Palazzo Vacchio). If it is, can you imagine the state it'll be in? Four hundred years ago, those guys painted on to damp plaster. And didn't always use tempera."

Maddox wasn't interested in an art history lecture.

"And a so-called Leonardo drawing on the rear of a painting at the Louvre?"

"The painting being 'Virgin and Child with St Anne'. But even that is proving incredibly difficult to prove; it's practically impossible to decide what it is. It could have been put there by some member of the Louvre staff years ago. But just a minute: how does Carlo fit into all this? I'm sorry, but I just can't see Carlo getting involved in Aldo's dodgy business. And just as important, how did he find out?"

"Did you know that your friend Carlo is a patron of several State galleries?"

"Of course. He's always talking – boasting, rather – about his work, influence; his wife is a trustee at the Duomo: a very devout woman. The fact that he knows little about the subject doesn't seem to bother him. Even with his family's history and a surname like his. But if Aldo is involved with a smuggling operation from his country's art treasures – where are they being smuggled to?"

"To the United Kingdom, initially." (That was how I got involved – the UK connection and my 'friendship' with Carlo, which Maddox had exploited.)

"What do you mean, 'initially'?"

"They will eventually end up, we believe, in Russia."

"Russia! How come? Oh, I see – some oligarch with his billions and his Mayfair mansion. How do they arrive in Moscow – in the diplomatic bag?"

"Your summation seems to be correct."

"Why do we allow these eastern barbarians into the country – buying football clubs and half the country's property?"

Maddox shook his head and finished his tea. I suddenly noticed that I hadn't touched mine. "From the hints on the disc…"

"You're not suggesting that Carlo also…"

"No, not at all." Didn't Maddox want to say to me that Carlo was also involved in Aldo's murky business? Apart from the fact that I wouldn't imagine for one moment that Carlo would be. The thought was ludicrous. *But then, why was he noting down every meeting with his son?*

The more I thought about it, the more bizarre the whole scenario looked. I said to myself, *What the hell are we discussing here? Is Maddox being deliberately confusing?* The thought that Carlo was running around Milan and Rome after his son Aldo was ludicrous. I was getting fed up with these speculations. I had given Maddox the info; what more did he want? I said:

"Anything else, Commander? For quite frankly I cannot believe Carlo Palladio has anything whatsoever to do with Aldo's dealings. I've known Carlo for a long time – yes, he and I are lovers (if you can call our twice-yearly meetings that), but we also have a mutual respect." I stood. "Look: I don't want anything more to with this. I've been spying on one of the few men I had learned to love. It has left a nasty taste in my mouth. I'm no angel, but this ends here."

Maddox faced me. He said quietly, "Dawn, you didn't say that when I offered you the opportunity."

Sod you, Maddox. You can stick your job. I'm tired of working for a pimp. But, of course, I didn't say that to him. Instead, what I did say was, "Well, where do we go from here. What more do you want from me?"

Maddox smiled. "Nothing, Miss Hope. You have done exceptionally well. As far as you are concerned, the case now moves to the next stage."

I looked at this tall, lean Scotsman in his tweed jacket and highly polished brogues, and thought, *I wonder what you really think of me, you Presbyterian?*

But now I had other problems on my mind and I turned them over as I walked home. They concerned my father. But before I faced that responsibility I couldn't get Carlo out of my mind. As I said earlier, he and I had met in Venice a few years earlier when my profession was perfectly respectable: highly qualified linguist (before I was conned into being an investigator for Revenue and Customs), was employed by an English businessman, attending the Biennale as a translator and P.A. So I trailed after Harris (I think that was his name) while he lorded it with his rich friends. I wasn't his mistress; it was strictly business; and anyway, he was accompanied by his wife – not that we saw much of her; she spent most of her time shopping and gossiping with the other wives. He had hired me from the secretarial and translation agency. I don't suppose he hardly noticed me. I did my job efficiently, and that was that. (At least we were staying at the Cipriani hotel.)

Anyhow, one afternoon I was left to myself, for which I was grateful. I sat in a quiet corner of the hotel lounge (if you can call a quiet corner of the Cipriana a lounge: looking back, I should have stayed in my room), reading (I think it was a paperback copy of *Mrs Warren's Profession*), and drinking coffee. I was almost aware of the bustle at the far end, near the reception desk, but of course taking no notice, when I felt a presence across from the armchair near mine. I was faintly annoyed, thinking, *They've got all the rest of the lounge, why disturb me?* I hoped it wasn't some tiresome Italian trying to chat me up. But after a few minutes, a voice said, in English:

"Good-day, signorina. You are English?"

Irritated, I looked up and stared at this well dressed, middle-aged Italian man. I said, in Italian: "Yes, I am. Who wants to know? I'm trying to read."

"I'm sorry if I disturbed you. My name is Carlo Palladio."

"Well actually, Signor Palladio, I am not interested. And where did you get such a ridiculous surname. Are you an architect?" That was where I made my mistake. Before I knew it, Carlo was telling me about his distinguished family, his sons and his daughter, and how he was some kind of patron at the Biannale (God, how these Italians do go on). Then he started to talk about the exhibits, and asked my opinion.

"You are interested in art, signorina?"

"Yes."

"Then you will be interested in all our art here at the exposition?"

"No. In my opinion it is a lot of pretentious rubbish."

He was taken aback by my frankness. It was then that I got a closer look at him. It was difficult to place his age. Forty? Forty-five? He wore a pearl grey suit, cream silk shirt, maroon silk tie; a red silk kerchief in his top left-hand pocket; highly polished brown loafers. He was clean shaven, square faced, wide-set brown eyes, long brown hair carefully cut.

Palladio replied, "You obviously do not like modem art?"

"Depends what you mean by 'modern'. Define your terms, signore. I don't consider blocks of wood or stone, or large blobs of paint on the floor to be art. Does that answer your question?"

He shrugged. He was out of his depth. I continued. "I have been walking these streets with my employer and his colleagues for the past five days – it is like touring one huge museum. This entire decrepit city is one huge work of art."

Carlo soon realised that he had better change the subject – or, better still, leave me alone; and I considered that was one way of getting rid of him. Instead he said: "What is your name, if I may ask?" (We were now speaking in English – and his was very precise.)

"Dawn Hope, aged 27, born in London, graduate in modem languages – like to know anything else?"

"I'm sorry if I seem intrusive…"

"That's OK. Now tell me, Mr Palladio: what made you sit next to me. Bored with life? Nothing better to do?"

He laughed. "I do your like your direct approach, Dawn. May I…?"

"Go ahead."

"I saw an attractive young woman, so I thought I would introduce myself." He raised his arms. "There!"

I didn't know what to reply to this outburst. I could hardly complain; he was being as frank as I was. Then he said:

"If you are free this evening, Dawn, would you dine with me, here at the Cipriani?"

I was so astonished (although I shouldn't have been) that, without thinking, I said, "Yes, I'd love to." What on earth made me say that? I wasn't used to being picked up in hotels – especially by middle-aged, suave Italians (or rather I was; but now I am expert at rebuffing). I came from a respectable academic family; hardly a blushing virgin, but a career girl. What would my father think…?

I got back to my room (probably the smallest in the hotel, but still too ornate for my taste) and an immediate feeling of panic – *what would I wear, did I have a pair of clean tights?* I had been walking in flats since I came here – *did I have heels to wear with the 'little black dress'?*

I hadn't been invited by my boss to eat in the Cipriani's restaurant; so I usually had supper in my room or ate in a trattoria near the Square. This was desperation time, so I went immediately to Reception and sought the aid of one of the girls behind the desk. She took me in hand and dragged me out of the hotel and into the street. I came back with a pair of Ferragamo shoes, two pairs of tights, and new underwear – all of which my new friend negotiated for me just as the store was closing ("Never pay full price in Venice, Miss Hope"). I got back to the hotel, thanked my new friend profusely, who winked, and wished me a pleasant evening (what did she think I was up to?).

I soaked in the marble bath with all the swanky smelly stuff and thought about all I had bought and said to myself – *Dawn Hope, what do you think are up to?* And: *You know damn well what you are up to.* I had used hotel shampoo and dried my hair, with the blow-drier, making my normal (natural) blonde fluff out, against its usual severe side parting. I said I would meet Carlo in the Gabbiano bar at eight o'clock, so I examined myself in the mirror – little black dress, high heels, and wearing my late mother's necklace. *OK, Dawn – let's do battle, for you look pretty good* (but my bra was a bit tight).

The Gabbiano bar, it seemed, was where all the great and good met before and after dinner. I walked through its elaborate entrance at exactly seven minutes past eight that evening. Carlo sprang to his feet from his chair near the gold drapes at the long window. The bar was half full; but neither of us attracted much attention, for which I was grateful. His greeting was elaborate, kissing my hand, and guiding me to a chair. He sat back in his chair, and said, "*Cara*, you look delightful!" He wore a rosebud in the left lapel of his tuxedo, which he removed and passed it to me. "An Italian rose for an English rose!"

I leaned across the table and retrieved it; then sat back and crossed my legs (my skirt rode just above my knee) and said, "Carlo, you are a fool – but I love it. Thank you." The thought suddenly came to me that it was such fun being with this man. When did I last have an evening out in a grand hotel with a handsome man – any man? I sipped at the glass of champagne (put in front of me as soon as I had sat down). I looked at Carlo over the rim: this man was too good looking and too rich for his own good – or mine, for that matter. A few hours ago, I was being the severe, standoffish Englishwoman (a condition endemic in female academics, being high-minded) not trusting embellishments from charming foreigners – now I was enjoying myself, and not giving a damn what was happening to me. Because *something* was certainly running through my veins; I was excited and feeling thrilled in this man's company.

We went into dinner at the hotel's Fortuny restaurant, which was like a pontoon set into the lagoon – crisp white cloths, candles glowing in little glass bowls, white-coated waiters bowing to Palladio, hovering round the table, menus like the dead-sea scrolls – oh, yes, it was all so perfect – the warm evening, the lights across the water. Carlo brought me down to earth.

"So, Dawn, what are you going to have? May I recommend the fish?"

"You may."

"Good! To start: seared lobster and orange sauce. OK?"

"Si."

"Then a little pasta with wild mushrooms?"

"Si."

"Ah! Roast turbot, lemon sauce?"

"Sounds delightful."

"Do you drink wine?"

"Of course."

"Excellent. I suggest a white from the Veneto – I have an interest in the vineyard."

So Carlo Palladio took charge, and was very attentive, and had the waiters running round me, pouring wine, and asking whether each dish was perfect, and of course I said 'yes'. All this sort of Latin fuss would have irritated and embarrassed me at one time – but now I was loving it. Eventually, we came to the end of the meal, fiddling with sorbets, when Carlo said:

"You have parents, Dawn?"

"A father. My mother died three years ago. I am an only child."

Carlo shook his head. "That is so sad!"

"My parents married late; my mother was forty when I was born. My father, like my mother, is an academic."

"A *professore*?"

"Yes; a philologist."

"Phil…?"

"An authority on the science of language."

"I see. Like you, he speaks other languages?"

"Several, plus Latin and Greek."

"Ah! A clever man with a clever daughter!"

"And you, Carlo, are a philogynist."

"And what is that!"

"A lover of women."

Carlo laughed out loud.

I loved showing off about my father; I had always put him on a pedestal. My mother used to say, "One always hears of fathers spoiling their daughters – but the reverse!" Then I used to hug my mother, who would say, "Off with you – go and finish those dishes."

Carlo said: "This is surely not your first visit to Italy?"

"No: after I graduated I spent six months at the University of Padova."

He grinned slyly. "And was the shrew tamed?"

"Very droll, Carlo. Incidentally, I think I'm just a little tipsy."

"Tipsy? Ah, you have perhaps had too much wine…"

(I thought: *Is he going to try to take advantage of me? Would I mind? Am I going to find my dress around my ankles…?*)

I sighed. "And the wine was lovely. And so was the dinner…"

Carlo interrupted me. "But it is now cool in the air. We'll take coffee in the salon."

So I allowed myself to be led away, slipping my arm through his. I caught sight of us in one of the mirrors in the long hallway: A sophisticated Italian male in evening dress and an English blonde in her 'little black frock'. Wearing my new heels, I was as tall as my escort. He waved me to the chair I had occupied earlier, then sat opposite me and beckoned a waiter. Silence. That kind of silence known as 'pregnant'; to think that Carlo would be lost for words!

I sipped my coffee – it was strong, which I usually dislike, but felt I needed it.

Suddenly, Carlo drained his cup, glanced at his wrist-watch, and said: "I am sorry, Dawn, but I must leave you."

"Oh."

He shrugged, stood, and then bent over me, kissing my hand. "I am truly sorry. But even this evening the time is not all my own. I hope you have enjoyed our time together?"

"It's been delightful, Carlo – thank you." Then he left. I got back to my room, hung up my dress, donned a gown, and slumped on the bed, feeling absolutely lost. And also – to my surprise – really rather cross. *Hang on, Dawn: what are you getting so fed up about? You had a wonderful evening with a handsome, well-mannered man, so why… oh, sod it!* I knew very well why. But I slept soundly (after all, I was a healthy young woman who had eaten and drank well) waking with no hangover at my usual time. This was my employer's last day; I knew that they were leaving on the noon-day flight, so all I had to do was pack my few belongings. I had decided previously that I would spend the remains of the morning wandering Venice, and join them at the airport.

After breakfast, I went to Reception to check whether there were any final messages from the Harrises: there weren't, just confirmation of the flight. I turned to leave, when my saviour from yesterday stopped me. "Signorina Hope. I have a package for you."

"For me?"

"Si." She gave me a sly look and smiled. I took it into the salon. The package was about as large as my hand, wrapped in purple tissue with a white raffia knot. I undid it carefully, eased the tissue and folded it neatly. Inside was a red leather box, tooled in gold leaf. I lifted the lid, exposing a gold bracelet set with rubies and white diamonds. I gasped. The light from the window made it flash in my palm. I removed the bracelet and slid it over my wrist. I still could not believe what I was holding. Then I saw the note. This was folded neatly at the base of the box. I spread the paper; it said:

My Dear Dawn,

I hope you will not be offended if I presume on our short acquaintance to offer you this gift, in memory of a delightful evening in your company.

We may not meet again, but I hope you will think of me when you wear it.

Carlo Palladio.

Pinned to the note were his business card and his private number in Rome and Milan.

Oh, Carlo, what have you done to me? Well, what follows shows what did happen to me – and all because of having dinner with an Italian millionaire who gave me a diamond bracelet. I wasn't some half-wit blonde; I was an educated woman with a first-class degree, and a father who was a distinguished scholar. But that didn't matter in the least once I got involved with Carlo Palladio.

***

But that adventure was all in the future. Even so, that first dinner with Carlo in Venice had me walking on air, and I hardly noticed my next-door neighbour, Susan Robinson, when she spoke just as she was leaving her home. She waved. "Oh, hello, Dawn. Have a good trip? How was Venice – still wet underfoot?"

"Only on the lagoon."

Susan grinned. "I'll bring Professor Hope's prescription home with me. OK?"

"Thanks, Susan."

Mrs Robinson was the pharmacist at the local medical centre – a kind woman in a nice family. Her husband was something to do with publishing the results of scientific research. I trod into the safety of the porch and opened the front door with my key. As I walked down the hall, my father's study-cum-library was on the right; behind that, a sitting room. To my left, a dining room that led on to the kitchen. The staircase to the upper two floors (plus large attic) was straight in front of me.

This house had been my home since I was a child. This was where my mother died. I still asked myself – why? One minute she was sitting on the sofa, reading; the next we knew, she had passed away, with no apparent reason. The death certificate said 'Heart failure'. She was healthy woman with no history of heart disease – and she just drifted away.

I called out to my father. "Dad – I'm home – the prodigal has returned!"

He hobbled to me on his walking stick. Had his mobility worsened? I kissed and hugged him. I said, "I hope you've been behaving yourself. What about the curvy Mrs Mills who supposed to keep an eye on you when I'm away?"

My father leant on my arm, as we went into the kitchen, and he said, "I have just brewed tea – the universal panacea." This was our routine when I came home from a business trip. "Now, daughter of mine let's have a look at you." I sat still dutifully. He said, "Dear me – you do look well; excellent colour in your cheeks. But were they overworking you?"

I shook my head. "Dad – don't fuss. But how about you – following doctor's instructions? And Mrs Mills keeping an eye on you?"

My father grimaced. "The woman's a menace – a dragon."

"I think she's got a soft spot for you, Dad. You want to watch your step there."

"Rubbish! God forbid that I should attract such a termagant."

I very nearly said something to the effect of, 'A monstrous regiment of women', but didn't want to push my luck.

Our house – as I mentioned earlier – had three floors. On the first floor was my father's bedroom (which he now reached via a stair lift); next to his sleeping quarters was a specially fitted bathroom. Next to his bedroom was a guest room (but my father didn't encourage visitors).

On the next floor was my bedroom and bath room. I had occupied that room since I was five years old – except for four years at Cambridge and postgraduate work at Padova – now I had returned from yet another business trip, and went through the familiar routine of unpacking, sorting laundry, checking my bed linens were fresh, opening windows, staring across the green, remembering when I used to cycle along the canal path to Little Venice. The ritual was always the same – even recalling the same thoughts.

But what of my father? I was convinced that his condition was worsening. It frightened me: the thought of losing my remaining parent; being alone; of returning home and finding my father... I shuddered and moved away from the window and closed the curtains. Standing under the shower, I followed the last part of my ritual... to 'wash all my troubles away.' I dressed in clean, pale-blue jeans and a white shirt – and slipped the magic bangle (as I now named it) over my left wrist. It looked incongruous in these surroundings, but what the hell. I wondered whether my father would comment. Sat at the desk in my room, I switched on my laptop and composed an email to Carlo It said:

Signorina Dawn Hope, M.A. is in receipt of your message and package and wishes to thank you most kindly. I shall be at this office email address and hope to be of further service to Signor Palladio. My telephone number is also enclosed.

I felt quite daring sending that to Carlo. What would he do – something very Latin-like, such as sending his Lear-jet and whisking me off to Positano? We would see. Until then, I had supper to prepare for my father and myself.

When I entered the dining room my father said, "I thought we would celebrate your homecoming with wine; I've decanted a bottle of claret."

"Dad, that would be lovely," I said, sounding surprised – it actually was part of the ritual.

So we sat companionably over our meal, drinking our wine, taking our time. I looked at him while he was eating: Professor Hope, my father; long face, carefully trimmed goatee beard, short haircut; his shirt clean and crisp, loosely knotted bow tie. He always had a good appetite; and enjoyed his wine. I had to admit he looked well at the dinner table that evening; one would not know that he was nearly crippled on the right side of his hip and leg with arthritis.

He looked at me over his spectacles and said: "Penny for them, daughter o' mine."

I took a sip of the claret, delaying an answer. "I was just thinking that you are still a handsome man – one would almost say distinguished. You could be quite a catch."

"I appreciate the terms 'still' and 'almost'. I suppose I should be flattered! But I've got enough on my plate with a cheeky daughter and my sister telling me what to do."

I said, "I think I've heard that before somewhere."

My father smiled. "Sorry; am I being a bore?"

"You are never that, Pops. Just the professorial lecturer occasionally."

"Don't be cheeky. And don't call me Pops."

I left my father in his study to his stamp collection after supper (what he called his pensioner's pastime. Which was nonsense; he had been collecting, swapping and buying stamps for 20 years) and cleared the kitchen. I was now on edge; what would Carlo's reaction be to my email? Was I making – or about to make – a fool of myself? I ran upstairs to my laptop, sat cross-legged on the bed and keyed in my mailbox. Nothing. Then I stopped: *Dawn Hope, you are behaving like an adolescent.* I switched off.

I came downstairs in my dressing-gown to the study; I leant over my father's shoulder. He was looking through a table magnifier; in his left hand was a pair of tweezers. They were holding a postage stamp. He turned it delicately, catching the light. "Now, what do you think of this?"

I stared through the magnifier. The picture was of a many-plumed bird, its tail sweeping low over its body; its head and beak staring, looking fierce. It was shown perched on some exotic tree, its multi-coloured plumage sweeping towards the ground. I said:

"It is exceptionally beautiful."

My father looked up. "Indeed it is. You know, Dawn, stamps are very often overlooked as works of art."

"He looks like a tough cookie, to me."

"Indeed he is: a crested barbet – *Trachyhyphonus vaillantii.*"

"I'm impressed: ornithologist as well are we?"

"Actually its name is on the envelope in which it arrived."

"You old fraud!"

"Not at all. I didn't try to deceive you. You assumed that I would know. But again, with your interest in art, would you agree with what said earlier?"

"Yes. I'll pay more attention in the future."

"Good, good!" He held my hand. "Also, I've just realised that I may have committed the sin of the enthusiastic amateur…"

"You mean going on and on…"

"Yes."

"Well, I can assure you that you never do. And by the way, have you taken your medication?"

"Ahhh – but Dawn, it makes me sleepy."

"That is one of its purposes. Kindly do as you are instructed."

I lay in bed on that June evening, the curtains pulled open, watching the blue-dark sky and thinking – and not being able to stop thinking – of Carlo Palladio. I got really cross with myself; had it been such a while since I had enjoyed the company of an intelligent and attractive man? As an only child, I could say that my psychology had made me something of a loner; but I did not have a nun-like existence; I was no blue-stocking like my Aunt Margaret. I was sociable, had friends of both sexes; I had played basketball at university and still did – but no man in my life for some time. Maybe I put men off? *Damn you, Palladio: you've upset my contented life.*

I dreamed that night that I was swimming in a lake; it was early evening; the water was warm; I was on my own in beautiful blue calm water. Then I realised that I was nude, as if I hadn't noticed this when I started to swim. I was alarmed, and started to panic, afraid that I would drown. Then a ringing bell woke me. It was my cell phone, blowing me out of the dream and the oneiric drama. My bedside clock read 2 a.m.

"Yes?"

'Dawn? *Cara*! I am sorry. I have woken you?"

I was still half awake, struggling to pay attention. "Carlo? God, man, do you know what time it is? Where are you?"

"Milan. I have only just read your message. I have been away – in Rome. Business. I am sorry again. Perhaps I will call later…"

"No. Don't, Carlo. Look: do you want us to meet again?"

A pause. "Yes, Dawn. As soon as possible. And you?"

"Yes. And don't keep me waiting, Carlo. I might fade away or enter a nunnery."

"I am not Hamlet. I will phone in two days' time. I promise." And he rang off.

So that brief conversation – in the middle of the night – changed the remainder of my life. I was also surprised at my own assertiveness. Now I *knew* I wanted that man. But I tried to put Carlo out of mind by working; the agency called me into its office off the Strand (one of many similar in WC2) with a choice of translating documents from Spanish into English (some real estate company in Marbella) or accompanying yet another business party to Madrid. Of course, I stayed in the office with the documents. I only hoped that my father didn't notice how jumpy I was at home.

At exactly 7 p.m. on the second day my cell-phone jingled. It was Carlo. He said,

"Are you free, Dawn? Now?"

"Well, yes. Where are you?"

"London."

"London!"

"Si."

"But where?"

"At a hotel in Knightsbridge – I always stay here. I have sent a car for you, English lady!"

I ran upstairs and changed quickly, and was in a panic about my hair and make-up. I put things in my capacious shoulder bag and ran downstairs. My father was in the sitting room, reading a newspaper. I said:

"Dad: I know this is awfully sudden; but I have to go out; I may not be back until the morning. Will you be all right?"

He was surprised, but didn't comment. "Of course, I'll be fine. Will you phone?"

"I promise." I kissed him. When I looked through the dining-room window, a large black Mercedes was waiting. The driver looked up as I closed the door behind me.

"Miss Hope?"

"Yes. Where are we going?"

"The Quest-Ritson Hotel. Mr Palladio asked me to collect you." I sank into a leather seat at the back of the car, took a deep breath and said to myself, *Here goes, Dawn Hope; straight down the primrose path…*

I woke suddenly, readjusting my mind slowly. Lying on my side, I opened one eye. My arm lay across the silk coverlet; from my position, all I could see was the diamond bracelet on my wrist. My arm was bare, as was the rest of my body. I could feel the soft sheet following my curves. I turned my head, so I could see across the room. Just under the long window was a red dress flung over a chair, now rather crumpled; on the floor, a white lace bra and a pair of miniscule white briefs. The pants had somehow got entangled with a Ferragamo shoe. Hmmm, I wonder how they got there.

I sat up and looked around the bedroom – or rather, the suite – and the sheet fell away from my shoulders, exposing my breasts, and smiled. A certain Italian gentleman had given me great pleasure by stroking and kissing my firm orbs. God: I could still feel him inside me. But where was he? Then I heard movement in the bathroom. I slipped out of the bedroom and peeped round the bathroom door. Carlo was standing in front of a long mirror, combing his hair; he wore a white fluffy robe.

He turned and looked at me. "*Ciao*, baby."

"You've got a nerve, Carlo Palladio: ravishing a girl then vanishing into your sanctuary."

He put the comb down and grinned. "You think I need sanctuary? You are not such a nice quiet English girl as I thought."

He looked me up and down, and I suddenly remembered I was naked, but I didn't move. "Do you like what you see, *signore*?"

"I adore what I see." He stepped forward and wrapped his robe around me; but I slipped under his grasp, and said:

"I am ravishingly hungry and I also need a shower. Order dinner, please. I shall be out in 15 minutes."

"Si, *signorina*."

But first, I kept my promise to my father and phoned home. Everything was OK there. Susan Robinson had called in with his medication. When I emerged from the bathroom (a nice clean girl) in another white fluffy robe, Carlo was still dressed in his. He looked at me. "Dawn…"

"That is I."

"…I need to tell you – I am sorry…" Suddenly I noticed that my clothes were no longer on the chair or floor.

"Carlo! Where's my dress and my smalls? All I can see are my shoes!"

"Your clothes are with the hotel staff. They will be returned early in the morning. Meanwhile, perhaps you would care to try these." He opened the wardrobe, and drew out a plum-coloured dress: I touched the fabric: it floated in my hands. He opened a drawer and I looked down at several sets of slinky silk underclothes plus pairs of tights in cellophane envelopes. Carlo said:

"I regret I did not have time to arrange more fresh clothes for you."

Before I could reply, there was a tap on the door and a waiter wheeled in a trolley laden with food. I suddenly felt rather a fool sitting crossed-legged on the bed, but Carlo, sitting on a sofa, just thanked him and put banknote in his hand. I sipped my wine and gorged on cold chicken, ham, potato salad, mayonnaise, rocket salad, and fresh rolls. I wiped my fingers on a napkin, then passed my wine glass for a refill. Carlo watched me with amusement; as before, he ate delicately, slowly – with finesse, even. But I was a healthy young woman with a strong appetite.

I said: "So, Carlo: this is absolutely wonderful – and thank you for the delightful clothes. But I ask myself: should I accept? Because if I did, would that make me your mistress. Hmmm?"

"You could never be anyone's mistress, darling."

"Perhaps not. But now we should put our cards on the table, *caro*. Where do we go from here? What do you want from me?"

"Or you from me…?"

I laughed. "In other words – from each other! Or is this just a one-night stand, Carlo? We've had a great time for a few hours, but…?"

He shook his head. "No, No, Dawn. I did not travel to England only for that!" He snapped his fingers. "If I wanted a young woman for one night I would have stayed in Rome and paid."

I thought that was a very Italian gesture, and was amused. I said: "The reason I am here, Carlo, is because I wanted you – I still do." I waved a hand. "This is all very lovely, but if you had suggested a back room in Hackney I would still have come."

"So would I. I love you."

Well, somebody had to say it eventually. So I repeated it. "I love you too, darling. But one thing."

"Yes?"

44

"You have a wife and family."

Carlo stood up and wandered round the room. "My wife," he said, "is... very devout." I immediately got a picture of a very wealthy man's standards of behaviour. One could have these peccadillos; but one must not bring them to public attention; the honour and reputation of the family must be protected.

"I understand you, Carlo. I am the soul of discretion. I don't want marriage but – I now realise I need a man like you. So do we understand each other?"

"Of course. It is fortunate that you are used to travelling in your professional life."

"In other words, if you say to me 'Please come to Milan or Rome or Sorrento' – I would do so?"

"Si. All your expenses would be paid."

"First class?"

"Of course."

"Then why don't you come back to bed?"

Chapter Two

Quest-Ritson Hotel, the following day

So I emerged from the lift and into Babylon. At least that is what it felt like as I walked into the foyer of the hotel. Is that what they called this area of marble floor and exotic plants, bronze statues of puttees, wearing very little (metamorphosed into lamp-holders) and cream leather chairs? I was freshly showered, my hair brushed neatly, wearing the red dress that had been cleaned and pressed by the hotel staff. I wore my new tights (Dior) and now-clean white smalls and Italian shoes.

So, what would Dawn Hope, B.A. (Hons) Cantab., M.A., London, call herself now? A kept woman? No, at least not yet. A whore or tart? Not sure about that: no money exchanged hands. Some very expensive clothes, yes, but an ardent male would do that for his lover. Even so, if this *affaire* continued (and I was going to make sure that it would), it looks as though Carlo Palladio would be spending a lot of euros on his… what about 'mistress'? He said that I would never be anyone's mistress. But money changes many circumstances. Let's leave it 'lover' for now, shall we?

Carlo was sitting in the dining room, looking through the window at the stretch of garden bordering Knightsbridge; through the plane trees one could see the traffic zipping down. But as soon as he saw me he stood. We kissed chastely on both cheeks. "*Buon giorno*, Dawn."

"And a very good morning to you, tiger." Carlo looked round quickly. But nobody in the restaurant noticed. I grinned at him: 'tiger' was not a term one applied to Carlo Palladio. He was a quiet and gentle lover; in all the time I knew him he never treated me with anything but respect. But I liked teasing him. As I sat next to him, a waiter hovered.

"Good morning, madam…?"

"Scrambled eggs, bacon, very crisp and a pot of tea, please."

Carlo was amused. "You are hungry this morning, *cara*?"

"What do you think after a night of debauchery, darling?" I put my hand under the table along his thigh. He removed it gently, smiling all the while, then slid his hand up my skirt. I nearly choked on the bacon. Served me right. "And anyway," I replied, "I'm a working girl." Carlo gave me a strange look. "No," I said, "not that... are you laughing at me, Carlo?"

We arranged to meet later that evening. But first I had to phone my father again; of course I was feeling a bit guilty – why, I don't know. He was used to my being away on business for two or three nights at a time. But even though my father always respected my privacy (and I his) I didn't like the idea that he would never know about Carlo. Did I suspect he wouldn't approve of my being with a married man; someone who had committed adultery with his daughter? But if the relationship continued with Carlo I couldn't keep it secret forever from Dad. *Oh, sod it*!

As I was leaving the hotel dining room and walking, obliquely, to the entrance, I noticed the manager's office door opening. A man (late 30s?) emerged followed by a young woman (early 20s?). She was very tall, at least six feet in her high heels; a brunette, smartly dressed and very good looking. I had only a glimpse of her as I approached the automatic doors – but as soon as I saw her I knew she was trouble. Why I should have the feeling about someone I didn't know and had not seen before, was puzzling.

As I walked to Hyde Park Corner Tube station, I couldn't get it out of my head. However, as I joined the morning crush the thought left me as I battled with the rest of the commuters on the Piccadilly line. I got out at Holborn (Covent Garden was nearer to the office, but I never alighted there: if the lift broke down, as it often did, there were a thousand stairs to climb), and walked the rest of the way to the Agency's offices.

I sat at my desk. There was still a pile of the Spanish documents needing translating.

"Morning, Frances. Beautiful day."

My boss looked up from the computer screen. "Good morning to you, Dawn. Indeed it is." She gave a sideways glance at the parcels I put against the wall. "Been shopping, have we? Those are very fancy labels."

"They are, aren't they? I've just found myself a millionaire boyfriend. He's always buying me lovely things."

Frances smiled. "Very funny, Dawn: you should be so lucky."

I thought that would be the best approach; now she would never believe I had met someone like Carlo – or was I just deceiving myself? I ploughed through the estate agents' documents from Marbella, and tried to tone down the purple prose when I put it into English. Then about 12.30 my cell-phone rang. I felt panic as I answered.

"Dad?"

"This is not your father, Dawn."

"Oh. Oh, yes."

"This is your lover, Carlo. *Come sta, cara.*"

"Very well, thank you," I said primly.

"Am I speaking to the same lady who sat astride me at midnight? The woman with the golden hair?"

I felt myself blushing horribly. I glanced quickly round the office, but everyone seemed busy. Even Frances wasn't looking in my direction. I said, "How may I help you?"

"You are working?"

"Yes."

"Can we lunch?"

"No, sorry."

"You are conscientious!"

"I hope so."

"Ahhh… Just think *cara*: we could have Parma ham, melon, a bottle of pinot grigio, then we could go to my room and I could undress you, then spend all afternoon make love. Si?"

If I let Carlo continue in this vein I would wet myself. "Well, thank you, Sir. I look forward to the meeting this evening." I crossed my legs and switched off the phone.

I left the office about four that afternoon with some of the Spanish papers in my document case. As I closed my front door behind me I heard voices coming from the sitting room,

Entering, I saw that my father had company: a woman. She was possibly in her sixties, slim, sitting very straight obliquely to my father on the sofa, dressed in a high-necked blue silk blouse and dark-blue skirt. My father said, "Hallo Dawn. You remember Anne, don't you?" (Yes: Dr Anne Holt, Department of Anthropology, at my father's university.)

"Oh, hallo, Anne: this is a nice surprise."

She smiled. "Nice to see you too, Dawn. Not running around Europe at the moment?"

"Thankfully, no." The coffee table was between them. On it was a pile of sandwiches and a sponge cake; they both had cups in their hands.

Anne said, "Cup of tea?"

"Er, no, thanks. I have to shower and change."

Dad looked up at me. "Anne raided the kitchen and made this sumptuous repast. Sure you won't join us?"

Well, all this looked very cosy, but I wasn't going to join in, so I left them to it. Well, well: had my father got himself a lady friend? I noticed he looked very spruce in his linen suit. Good luck to him. Raiding the kitchen eh? Hmmm, not too sure about that…

After I showered and shampooed I did a very daring thing; I painted my toenails red. I sat on the bed wriggling my feet, waiting for the harlot's colour to dry. Then donned a set of silk undies Carlos bought: a camisole top and French knickers in pink. I giggled. They were the sort of things my grandmother would have worn. Quite sexy, though. But the plum-coloured silk dress (Robert Cavalli!, straight from Via della Spiga, Milan, no doubt) was sensational; cross-over V-neck, to emphasise my bosom and the skirt flowing out in thin silk layers. Madonna eat your heart out. I thought I might as well go the whole hog, and wore a deep red lipstick. I swirled around my room. God, Dawn: you had better watch your step tonight, girl. The black Mercedes arrived exactly on time as before. I stuck my head round the sitting room door; Dad and Anne were still seated opposite each other, chatting, but the tea things were no longer there. I said:

"Bye, Dad."

They turned and smiled. My father said: "Have a nice evening."

Hmmm. He seemed not to be very interested in what I was doing – and Anne winked. Sumptuous repast indeed! I walked into a lovely June evening, carrying my valise and a paisley pashmina. Joseph, the driver, got out of the car. At that moment, my next-door neighbours' younger son, Jonathan, turned the corner; he was accompanied by a leggy girl with frizzy hair. They were both carrying gym bags.

"Hallo, Jonathan." He was a bit startled, possibly because the girl seemed to be talking nineteen to the dozen.

"Oh, hi, Dawn. You look a bit slinky; is this your transport? Wow. Sexy or what?"

The girl frowned and nudged him. Then he turned his attention to the Mercedes.

I said to her, "We know each other, don't we? Rebecca Fairfax, isn't it?"

"Oh, gosh, yes; our team played yours at the basketball tournament."

"And you beat us."

"Oh dear, yes; so we did. That is an absolutely super dress you're wearing, and the bracelet. Are your shoes Italian?"

"All of it's Italian. Inside and out."

"Heavens: really? It looks terribly expensive."

Jonathan interrupted. 'Come on, Rebecca – don't be such a nosy mare." I heard them arguing as I got in the car:

"Jonathan, don't be so rude. I hope your mum has made some more of those chocolate brownies."

"Don't you think of anything else except food?"

"But, Jonno, we've been training all afternoon and I'm starving!"

"And don't call me Jonno."

I sat back in the voluptuousness of the Mercedes, and thought, *Well, those two adolescents seem to getting along all right.* I closed my eyes. And so did my father and Anne.

Hmmm. *What's the matter with you, Dawn? You couldn't be jealous, by any chance, could you? Rubbish.* I would be only too pleased if Dad had some nice female companionship. But where were Carlo and I going? All this attention – designer dresses, swanky hotels, and chauffeur-driven limos – was lovely. But he lives in Italy and I live in London. I always thought of myself as essentially English. All right, anywhere I go in Western Europe I could communicate with the natives and 'fit in', but I was always relieved to be home.

It had passed through my mind (but not too often) of perhaps getting married and having children. In two or three years I would be thirty years old; is that when career women start watching their biological clock? I hadn't considered that before. *Before what? You know very well, Dawn Hope. Oh, shut up.*

As I entered the lobby of the Quest-Ritson hotel, I saw Carlo speaking to one of the receptionists. He looked in my direction, came and kissed me, but seemed distracted. He said, "Shall we have a drink on the terrace? It is a beautiful evening."

"That would be lovely."

We sat side by side overlooking the garden. At the far edge of the lawn plane trees threw their shadows across the greenery. We sat in silence, sipping vermouth. Then he said, "I have to return to Milan tomorrow."

"Oh."

"I am sorry, Dawn."

"Well, of course you had to return eventually." He put his glass on the table and looked at me.

"You look wonderful in that dress."

"Thank you, *signore*. A rather special gentleman bought it for me."

"Ah. He has excellent taste."

"Especially in blondes."

Carlo laughed; so did I.

Then suddenly I said, "I have to leave, now."

"What. Why?"

"Do you have your room key?"

"Of course…"

"Then give it to me – now." I grabbed the key and my valise and ran from the room, leaving Carlo opened-mouthed and alarmed. I let myself into Carlo's suite and dashed into the bathroom. *Damn, damn, damn!* I hung my dress in the wardrobe, did what I had to do, then lay on the bed in a white, fluffy bathrobe. I heard Carlo enter; he had removed his jacket and had pulled his tie from his collar.

'Dawn! *Ecco qua! Come sta?*' He sat on the edge of the bed and held my hand.

I said, "Sorry about that, Carlo. It's rather embarrassing, really."

"How is that? You are sick?"

"No. No. The time of the month caught up with me suddenly. At least you haven't made me pregnant."

Then it dawned on Carlo what the hell was happening. He laughed out loud. "I see! But you are OK?"

"I'm fine, of course. It was all rather embarrassing. Sorry to cause a fuss."

He spread his hands. "It is only nature! Do you want to have dinner here?"

I slid off the bed. "No, darling. Let's eat out. OK? Just pass me my dress, please."

We strolled down Sloane Street to the square, and found an Italian restaurant, which Carlo knew. So on that last evening we ate prosciutto and salad with olive oil and sea salt and green olives and smoked fish and drank Chianti, taking our time, just letting the evening pass by. I looked at Carlo, and thought, *You are really rather a handsome man, Carlo Palladio. I do have quite strong feelings for you. Is it love? Am I in love with this man? We're going to have to talk about this affaire…*

I said: "Tell me more about your wife, Carlo."

He lowered his wine glass, and was silent for a moment, then said: "Dawn, there is something you must understand about families like mine in Italy."

I thought I knew exactly what he was going to say. Marriages were arranged between two powerful and/or rich families in a quiet manner. The sentimental attachments we look for in Britain were an irrelevance. The couples had a duty to forge an alliance; have children and show a respectable front, such as attending mass regularly and support the Church's charities generously. A husband may eventually take a mistress, but he would be very discreet.

And that of course is what Carlo said. Did he think I was an ignoramus? That I wanted – Heaven forbid! – to break up his marriage? What I did reply was, "It all sounds positively medieval, as if you were a d'Medici." He shrugged. I laughed, and said, "Let's leave and walk, I want you to listen to me." But when we got outside, we just walked hand-in-hand and didn't speak until we approached the Quest-Ritson.

We sat in the now empty lounge, drinking coffee. I said: "I have to ask you, Carlo: when you return to Milan tomorrow, where does that leave me? Do we forget our *affaire*? You said your wife was devout – would she be very distressed if she knew you had a lover?"

"I don't want to forget, Dawn. I cannot walk away from what we have found. Would you accept me as I am – is that too much to ask of you? If so…"

"*Your wife, Carlo!*'

He shook his head. "To answer your question – no, I don't believe she would." He stood and looked out of the window. It was now quite dark, but the points of light from hotels and cafes still shone. "Dawn: I have a suggestion."

"Yes?"

"Come back to Milan with me, Dawn, please."

"You mean permanently?"

"Si."

"No."

"I could give you a good life, *cara*. A career in one of my companies. Plenty of money – whatever you wish."

I remembered the conversation – the 'practical' arrangements that we looked forward to. That now seemed unreal. But recalling them now meant that I might be accepting them. Even so, I wasn't going to let him get away with it that easily. And what was it I said about 'making damn sure our liaison would continue'?

"I've never heard anything quite so selfish. Am I supposed to abandon my father, friends, my life here just so you would have a lover when needed? Sorry, Carlo: *la dolce vita* doesn't appeal. If that is all you have to say, I'm leaving right now." I started to walk away – *how dare he*!

He stopped me. "Dawn, please. I was wrong. I'm sorry. I have offended you."

I sat down again, my anger slowly subsiding. I could taste the strong coffee at the back of my throat. I said, "Carlo, darling, please…"

"Yes?"

"Could you get me a glass of cold white wine?"

Surprised, he walked out of the lounge. Five minutes later (and I had panicky feelings when he didn't return immediately) he came back with a waiter and a half bottle of Dom Perignon. Well, you could say what you liked about Carlo, but he certainly had style. I took a gulp of the beautiful wine and looked at him. *Oh, Carlo…*

We sat in silence for a while. Eventually, someone had to take the initiative. So I swallowed my pride (and thinking of his male Italian pride) and said:

"Look, darling, I think I have a solution. We still want to see each other, yes? Then let us meet just when we can. I will phone or email you, or you do the same. If you are in London, I will come to you. If you are in Italy, or France, or whatever, you send for me. I promise you I will do my utmost to come. What do you say?"

He grinned, delighted. "Oh, yes, Dawn. Yes. But?"

"But? What but?"

"I will cover all expenses. Air travel. All!"

Well, I could hardly say no, could I? So that was how our affaire continued, though I like to think that it was more than that. We loved each other; that was the truth. Even so, there was the niggling thought at the back of my mind that eventually it would have to end someday. I am sure that Carlo did not have other lovers; neither did I. But during the following weeks and months my life changed, and indirectly it was because of my meetings with Carlo. The following account shows how a nice, well-educated girl from the professional class turned into something of a *femme fatale*.

A piece of advice if you become a *fatale*: Unlike me, keep your legs crossed.

Chapter Three

London: Maida Vale

Sunday morning, and a week later I was lying in my own bed alone, waking to thoughts – of what? My rising tide of consciousness left me with pictures of last weekend flashing across my mind, most of which were exceptionally satisfying; and then starting a working week without the thought of Carlo Palladio spoiling yours truly. Just because I was an only child did not mean that my parents always indulged me. My mother, especially, had firm principles of how a teacher should conduct herself with children – and that included her daughter. What it was all about as far as I was concerned was that my parents knew I was clever, that I was as excellent at languages as my father: but it did not mean that I was allowed to go on any ego-trip. Diligence and self-discipline were the rules in our household.

But I always remember a happy childhood. It was privileged, of course: I was privately educated up to the time when the sixth form loomed. My parents decided that I should be shoved out of the nest into the State system at that stage so I would have to 'rub shoulders in the market-place', as my mother called it. At that time, I was being a rather rebellious adolescent – hormones all over the place, etc.; and tried the usual game of playing one parent off on the other. That didn't work, at least never with my mother: and not always with my father.

My best memory of my mother was when I was about ten or eleven years old. We were on holiday in Brittany, along that rocky coast, and had hired a *gite* in August. She and I would paddle around the rock pools, searching for *fruits-de-mer* (as she insisted I call them). What we caught was hardly a feast; but we both shrieked with delight every time we netted a crab or prawn. My mother was always giggling and holding my hand on that happy holiday. At night, when I was lying in bed, I would ask her to read to me; she would say, "Wouldn't you rather read your books to yourself, darling?" But I remembered when I was small, when she used to read to me and I would fall asleep.

So I would say, "Mummy, read *The Tyger Voyage*."

"You haven't brought that with you, have you!" And she would laugh.

So that Sunday morning waking, stretching, yawning and slipping out of bed wearing one of the slinky bits of nightwear that Carlo had bought me, it brought me down to earth. I drew the curtains aside and stared from my eyrie down to the parkland. I had two things to face today: speaking to my father and entertaining my Aunt Margaret (Dad's sister) to lunch. It was all to do with guilt, of course: keeping my big secret from Dad. He had never asked me about any private life I might have; boyfriends, or whatever. But I had always talked easily of friends, both male and female. My parents had encouraged me to invite them to the house, right from when I was small. So he must be wondering why I had been so tight-lipped during the past few days. *Ah, well, Dawn Hope, remember that conscience doth make cowards of us all – so go and disprove it.*

I watched my father spread butter on the slice of wholemeal toast, exactly to the edges, then he picked up a clean knife and spread marmalade diagonally down the middle. This done, he repeated the process with honey on the other side, so they were an exact match. He sliced the toast down the middle, so now he had a piece with honey and a piece with marmalade.

He said: "So, which should I eat first, Dawn?" He smiled at me.

I said: "Would it not have been easier, Dad, to make two slices of toast – one of honey; the other with marmalade?"

He raised a finger to me. "Ah, but then there would be no aesthetics involved, so lessening the pleasure. *Vous compris?*"

I wasn't going to play that game; I needed to speak to him seriously. "What pretentious rubbish!" I poured two cups of coffee. "Dad?"

"Yes, love."

"Would you listen to me, please. I need to tell you something."

"Of course: I won't interrupt."

"Well, actually, Dad, I want to apologise…"

"Really? Why is that? Sorry… won't interrupt again."

That put me off my stride for a moment. But I said: "I've been a bit grumpy all week. Sorry."

My father shook his head, as if he hadn't noticed. I continued: "It goes back to when I was in Venice. I met a man – an Italian, very charming. Took me to dinner. He was very polite and proper."

My father smiled at the word 'proper'. I continued, "He came to London. I felt I had to see him again, so I did. Those two nights I was away, I was with him. We fell for each other…"

"May I now interrupt, Dawn?"

"Of course."

"Is there a problem?" (He was ahead of me.)

"Yes. He's married, and older than me."

My father was silent for a full minute, staring out of the kitchen window. *God*, I thought, *he doesn't approve. What am I going to say?* He eventually faced me, and I felt as if I were five years old. "Can you tell me more, Dawn?"

So I explained about Carlo and his family, and his wife, and his children, and his position as a very wealthy man in Italian society. I also explained the arrangement Carlo and I had come to. My father thought for a moment, then looked at me again.

He said: "I suppose I always hoped that you would eventually marry and have children, even though later, perhaps like your mother and I! But it's your life, love. I don't want you to get hurt, Dawn! Are you sure that you are satisfied with that sort of relationship? What if you become pregnant? Or if he leaves you. Hmmm?"

"I don't know, of course, but I'm willing to take that chance. You don't think, Dad, that I want him for money, do you? I'm not a prostitute!" I was getting angry. And my father was shocked.

"Dawn – I would never think that of you!" He sighed. He looked as if he was in pain. I felt awful. *The wages of sin...* Then he said firmly: "Dawn, whatever you decide, it is not for me to judge you. All I will say, is, I'll always be here for you. All right?"

I leaned across the table and hugged him. "Thanks, Dad." I also knew that he would never refer to me and Carlo again – and never mention it to anyone else. But now there was Aunt Margaret and lunch to think about. Why people make such a fuss about Sunday lunch is beyond me – day of rest, indeed! One would think that of the one day in the week where one did not feel an obligation, Sunday would be it: lying in bed until midday; scattering newspapers all over the sitting-room; watching moronic programmes on TV... which could equally applied to Christmas, of course. The French and Italians have the best idea: they eat out at Sunday lunchtime.

Wait a minute; am I just being a miserable cow? Just because I hadn't heard from Carlo? Of course. So, Dawn Hope: don't be a miserable cow. Then my mobile rang while I was in the kitchen, in the middle of preparing lunch. I listened for nearly ten minutes without interrupting (except for the occasional 'Yes' or 'No'). I'll give you ten thousand guesses as to who that was.

Then the doorbell rang. Margaret. My father was hobbling down the hall; but my aunt had let herself in. (Greetings down the hallway: "Edgar, dear! How are you?") I was taking a few deep breaths by this time – a literal breathing space. I followed their voices to through the sitting-room on to the terrace, where my father had spread a white cloth over the round iron table.

He had placed knives and forks and mats on the cloth in his usual meticulous manner. The tall clear wine glasses sparkled in the sunlight; he was opening a bottle of white wine. Aunt Margaret turned as I approached. "Dawn: there you are, dear!" I always thought it odd that Margaret always addressed me and my father by that term; as if we were minor characters out of a novel by Trollope. My aunt was a tall woman – at least five-ten in her stockinged feet (unusual in our family; my father was barely five-eight; but at least I was his height). Slim, almost thin, Margaret always stood straight, legs apart, head up in what I always thought of as my headmistress as a child. I was a bit scared of her when younger. Now she stood, with a wine glass in her left hand, head held high, and said: "Well, now, you two – what have you been up to? Tell me all the news."

My father once remarked that, when we entertained my aunt, she always asked the same question. He said it reminded him of Queen Victoria's remark when being spoken to by Gladstone: "As if he were addressing a public meeting."

Margaret continued, looking particularly at me: "Still running around Europe, Dawn?"

"Not all of it, Margaret; just the civilised areas."

She said, "I can't quite understand why these businessmen require a translator. Surely the people with whom they are doing business have their own English-speaking staff?"

"No doubt," I said. 'But when I attend meetings we do not mention that I am a translator. All they see is someone taking notes – that's me. As far as they are concerned I'm just another PA. So when, for example, we are doing business with a French company and someone from their office is speaking some kind of English, I understand every word, every aside to their colleagues. They'll be speaking off the cuff. You'll be surprised what we learn."

"It seems a very convoluted way of conducting a meeting!"

"Ah, Margaret: business is all about two things: Money and information. The more information one has, the bigger the returns."

As we sat on the terrace, I could feel the sun on my back through the thin silk of my dress: I moved my chair. When I brought the food through, Margaret was cross-examining my father about his health. He dismissed her questions. "Have a glass of wine; I think you will find this Kiwi sauvignon blanc rather good."

My aunt was no gourmet; she would eat anything put in front of her. But she was a wine lover like the rest of the family. "Lovely, Edgar, lovely." We were having what my father called a 'collation' – in other words, cold ham, chicken, potato and green salad, etc. Which, combined with the summer day, got me out of cooking. While I was eating, I couldn't keep the phone call out of my head; consequently, I made short polite rejoinders to the general conversation. Margaret looked at me quizzically. She said:

"That is a very pretty dress, Dawn."

"Thank you, yes."

She glanced at my left wrist. "Are those diamonds in your bracelet?"

I was getting fed up with this. "Yes. It was a present from my Latin lover: he buys me designer dresses and diamonds. We shall be spending next weekend on his yacht in Monte Carlo harbour."

Margaret raised her eyebrows; my father frowned. "In other words, mind my own business?"

"Got it in one, auntie."

She removed herself from this slightly embarrassing situation by addressing my father. I poured myself another glass of the white wine. She said:

"Well, Edgar: are you doing anything with yourself?"

My father smiled. "As a matter of fact I am. They've asked me to revise my commentary on the Codex, in light of the latest findings."

Margaret brightened at this. "That is splendid, Edgar, dear. Are you looking forward to the work?"

My father looked at me. "Very much so: and perhaps some unpaid secretarial help."

So that was all right. Back to ancient Greek again. Margaret sat back in her chair and drained her glass. She said: "Well, I have some news for you."

"Tell us, Margaret; tell us."

"I've been asked to chair a Royal Commission on the future of higher education."

We were both taken aback; Margaret was a few years younger that my father. Even so, I expected that she was thinking of retiring.

I said: "It's about time someone sorted it out. And I can't think of anyone better." I meant what I said. Margaret was obviously pleased at our reaction: for a formidable woman, she seemed somewhat embarrassed at that moment.

"There's something else, actually."

"Oh, what's that?"

"They want to put me in the House of Lords."

My father exclaimed, "Good heavens, Margaret: are we going to have Lady Hope in the family? A real live baroness?"

My aunt waved that aside. "You know what governments are like: it goes with the job." Even so, I found it faintly amusing that a member of the family should ally itself – however tenuously – with a particular Government. I had never heard of any of them make a remark supporting any Party, Tory or Labour; except to criticise their lack of intelligence. But then, we were all scholars, and questioning was second nature. My father and Margaret moved to the sitting-room with their coffee cups. I left them to it.

In my bedroom, I lay on the duvet and recalled the phone call from Carlo. I felt slightly dizzy – and I don't think it was the wine: a further assignation had been planned.

"Dawn, *cara, cherie*? Carlo: are you free to speak?"

"Of course: why shouldn't I?"

"Can we meet?"

"Please! When? Soon?"

"Next Thursday."

"Where? Milan?"

"No, France."

"France! Where?"

"Ah ha! My little secret!"

"Carlo! Please stop teasing!"

"I have made the arrangements. Go to Heathrow by ten a.m. Terminal 4. Check in at the British Airways first class desk. Your reservation has been made."

"But, Carlo, I don't know where…"

"Trust me."

"But you are an Italian male." (He laughed down the line.)

"Will you take a chance with Carlo? Your lover?"

"Of course. I love you."

"I love you too. *Ciao*, baby."

Still lying on my bed, I tried to read (a life of Walter Sicke: all those weird paintings in Camden Town), but I couldn't concentrate. But next morning (Monday) was the start of a working week. So promptly at 8.30 I phoned Frances at the Agency. "Hi, Frances. Dawn Hope. Did you have a nice weekend? Lovely day."

"You sound chirpy. Good morning. More to the point, did you finish those documents?"

"I burned the midnight oil. All day Saturday and well into the darkening hours; I felt like a Romantic poet."

"Most of who were a pain in the bum. First question: how's your Portuguese?"

"Portuguese! We haven't touched that for a while… why do you ask?"

"I've had request from the Home Office for a document translator – what do you think?"

"Depends on the content. But, yes; I can do that." I didn't want to sound too enthusiastic; working for the Civil Service – all that red tape, etc. (Knowing what I know now, I should have run a mile from the task). Bureaucracy made me think of Aunt Margaret – the 'Future of Higher Education', eh? Well, if anyone could control a committee, she could. It would require a mixture of *audax et caudus*. It was all very well looking to the future, but with all those dumbed-down 'A' levels, what do they expect? 'Media Studies', indeed!

However, I got to the office about 9.30. Frances Brooke, the co-owner of the agency, was sat behind her desk, with three piles of files in front of her. Frances was in her late forties, a biggish woman with broad shoulders, but she also had a lovely heart-shaped face; a good skin; wide, humorous mouth – and hard grey eyes. She wore her spectacles on a cord round her neck. As I walked into the office, her husband, Harry, was stood behind her.

"Ah," she said, "the fashionista!"

I was wearing a red designer dress with square neckline and fitted waist – and red Italian shoes (no diamond bracelet today). Harry said: "You know, Dawn, I sometimes have fantasies about you when you have left the country." (*God*, I thought, *is my slip showing?*)

"Oh, yes, Harry?"

Frances looked up at her husband. "Tell us more, dear."

Harry sat on the edge of his wife's desk "Well, Dawn: I can imagine you in St Petersburg, meeting an attaché from the British Embassy. It is winter; you are stood shivering in the entrance to the Hermitage – suddenly along comes this handsome young officer from the security police, and he hands you the secret plans. Suddenly, you are surrounded by militia and you die in each other's arms…"

"Good heavens, Harry – what an imagination you have. But what happened to the attaché from the British Embassy."

"Oh, he didn't turn up."

I said to Frances, "Apart from the fact that I have never been to Russia in my life – what have you been putting in his coffee?"

Harry said: "Phenobarbitone."

Frances shooed her husband away, and she and I got down to business. I said, "I hope it isn't one of those jobs at the Crown Court, translating for some poor wretch, and being kept hanging about until the case comes up. If it is, I am saying no. They are just not worth the effort, Frances – and the pay is crap. And by the way, I shall be out of the country from Thursday until next Monday. A *petite vacance*.'

Frances looked at me before replying. She said: "Is anything more you wish to say before I pronounce sentence, Miss Hope?"

Oh, God. I backtracked. "Oops, sorry, Frances. Rather rude of me. Please continue." (*That's the second time, Dawn Hope: your father ticked you off for being rude to Margaret.* And I had replied, *Isn't it interesting, that plain-speaking people don't like it when you do the same to them?*)

"Thank you. If you had let me, I was about to say that you are not wanted in Court. You have to present yourself to the Home Office in person to somebody call Maddox; take some form of ID, so they know who you are."

"Sounds spooky."

Frances glared at me. "Look, Dawn: this little job could do my Agency a lot of good, so please be on your best behaviour. Do this for me – us – Dawn, please?"

"Of course I will. I won't let you down. Sorry about the flippancy. When do they want me?"

Frances glanced at the wall clock. "In one hour thirty minutes from now."

"Are you sure you are looking at the right clock?' (There were several clocks on the office wall, relating to different time zones.)

"Perfectly sure. Off you go; better get a sandwich and coffee. You don't know how long you'll be."

"But this Maddox might take me to his gentleman's club in St James's."

"Pigs might fly. Buzz off."

So I did as I was bid. And after hurriedly eating a cheese roll and slurping a latte at the scruffy Italian cafe round the corner, I took a taxi to SW1 (*don't forget to ask for a receipt, Dawn*). The Home Office is situated in Marsham Street; it is a horrible glass building, sixties style, with a thumping great metal sign announcing itself. I removed my Gucci shades (those, with the red dress and red shoes, completed the power dressing) pushed the double door and looked round. There was a middle-aged, old soldier type in a dark-blue uniform and shiny black shoes standing behind a desk. He said:

"Good morning, Miss. Can I help you?"

I said Good morning to him, gave my name, and said I had an appointment with Mr Maddox. He picked up a phone, and I sat in one of the black faux leather chairs. I glanced at my watch: I was five minutes early. And I waited. And waited. I said to the man, "Did Mr Maddox say how long he was going to be?"

"Afraid not, Miss."

I glanced at my watch yet again. I had been sat in the entrance for thirty minutes; nobody kept me waiting that long. I stood and reached in my shoulder bag. I gave the man a business card, and said, "Please inform Mr Maddox that I can't wait any longer – I can be contacted at that number."

The old boy seemed taken aback. "But, Miss…"

"No 'but's, chum. Just give him that."

I was so cross; here was I trying to do Frances a good turn for the Agency, and some fool of a civil servant didn't even have the courtesy to say how long he would keep me waiting. So I walked quickly down the pavement in the direction of the Tate Britain – that would put me in a better mood. But that was going to be a long walk, and it was getting to be the warmest part of the day; I could feel my dress starting to stick to my shoulder-blades. Damn. Then my cell-phone rang.

"Yes?"

"Dawn Hope?"

"Who are you?"

"Duncan Maddox."

"Oh."

"I wish to apologise for keeping you waiting like that. Where are you, Miss Hope?"

"Five minutes' walk from your office."

"I'll meet you in reception. Agreed?"

"Very well." I don't know why I agreed; not wanting to let Frances down, I suppose.

Duncan Maddox was a tall, rangy, middle-aged man. He wore a light-weight tweed suit, a crisp white shirt and a club tie. His brogues were highly polished. My first impression was that he would look more at home at the Horse of the Year Show than a government office. However, he was politely apologetic as we shook hands. As we walked down a corridor, he explained that the document was in rather a fragile condition. "I hope," he said, "that won't cause too many difficulties for you?"

"We shall see."

He held the door open for me; we entered a pleasant-enough office – pale green walls, comfortable high back chairs. There was a metal desk covered in dark-red fabric, with two Angle poise lamps. He picked up a telephone that sat on a small filing cabinet and instructed someone to bring in the document. A few minutes later a young man appeared with a piece of A4 paper in a plastic sleeve. I opened my shoulder bag and retrieved a folding table magnifier with built-in daylight-simulated bulbs.

Techniques my father had taught me when studying his stamp collection.

Maddox watched me as I placed rubber-tipped tweezers by the side of the sheet.

He said: "Would it disturb you if I stayed, Miss Hope?"

I smiled. "Not at all – as long as you are good and quiet. And please call me Dawn." (I couldn't resist that.) He didn't reply. It didn't need the magnifier to see that the piece of paper had had some rough handling. It was certainly written in Portuguese – but not all of it. But I was going to keep quiet about that for the moment. I said:

"This sheet has been in the water, probably for some time, Mr Maddox?"

"Yes, Dawn: sea water."

Now I was getting the fundamentals sorted out. A lot of the printing was faded – especially so with the non-Portuguese words. I worked slowly through the first part of the document.

And then realised what I was reading. I lifted my eyes from the magnifier and turned to Maddox. "This is a bill of lading – or at least part of it, isn't it?"

He smiled. "Well done, Dawn!"

I replied: "And if I am not mistaken, the other characters are Lithuanian?"

"We could only guess."

"Like me! But look: I'll write my guess. OK? You really need my father."

So this is what I wrote: laivas astyje 21.00hrs. Krovinio perdavinas 24 hrs.

"Thank you, Dawn. I'll pass it on."

"You sound as if you knew that all along, Mr Maddox: so what is going on?"

Not in the least abashed, he replied: "Don't jump to any conclusions, Dawn. Let me explain. My man who looked at this document initially *assumed* they were; but it was just a guess."

"So what stopped him going further?"

Maddox smiled again. "He didn't have your expertise, and he is not here because his wife has just had a baby."

"Ah. So he's got his priorities right; you'll want me to carry on?"

"If you would."

"Of course. I'm sorry: I didn't mean to be difficult. It's just…"

"Good! I'll get my secretary to find you some coffee and sandwiches."

"Thank you."

What a strange conversation that was. I was to find that Maddox brought out the best and worse in me. So I ploughed through this seemingly innocuous document, with its waterlogged writing. The other problem was that the detailed lists on the page were in a small typeface. Even so, the lists (in Portuguese) seemed innocent enough; exporting port, cork, linens, etc. It was the Lithuanian that didn't seem to make sense – and why Lithuanian, for God's sake? Eventually, after numerous cups of coffee (I rarely eat when I'm working) I translated the document; but Lithuanian is not one of my languages; so they were guesswork. That would be up to somebody else in this strange department.

I glanced at my wristwatch: 6.30 p.m. *Good heavens, I'd better phone my father.* When I had put his mind at rest, Duncan Maddox came in. He was accompanied by the same young man. I looked him over: medium height, dark hair brushed back from his forehead; square face, brown eyes, sharp, long mouth. He stood lightly on the balls of his feet. He was dressed conventionally enough in a dark blue suit; but he looked like a tough nut.

Maddox said to him, "File it please, John."

"Of course, sir." His English was 'top drawer' – so what? Another well-bred hooligan with an education. I started to pack my shoulder bag; magnifier, tweezers; and searched among the debris for my sunglasses (Tampax, clean white cotton briefs, moisturiser, tissues, make-up sachet, and condoms). Maddox guided me to the front of the building, where I left my Visitor ID. He shook my hand.

"Goodbye, Dawn, and thank you for your diligence. Mrs Brooke will no doubt send in her invoice. I hope we will meet again."

"Goodbye, Mr Maddox." *Meet again? I hope not. And remember that I get paid from the time I entered Frances's office.* I strode down Marsham Street, wondering where the nearest Tube station was, or hoping to catch a taxi – but maybe not at this time in the evening. I suddenly felt a chill, and looked at the sky; black clouds were forming from the west; then I felt the first spots of rain. I dug in my shoulder bag for my 'telescope' brolly. Then the heavens opened, and I dashed under the nearest shelter, which happened to be an office block with an overhanging entrance. By that time, the top and hem of my dress were soaked, and I was shivering. I suddenly felt very alone, just watching the rain fall in sheets.

Oh, sod it! After about ten minutes I was feeling very miserable. As I was staring across the road a dark-blue (or black, I couldn't really see through the rain) Audi drew up at the edge of the pavement. The passenger window slid part way down.

"Dawn Hope come on, get in!"

I didn't care who it was – I just wanted to escape. I slammed the car door behind me, and looked at my rescuer: it was Maddox's assistant, John. John what? He said:

"You OK, Dawn?"

"Yes, and thank you for coming to my rescue, John…?'

"John Hibbert." He smiled thinly. "I have orders to take you home safely."

I didn't reply at first; I was too conscious of my wet – now nearly transparent – dress. *Oh, Dawn, why didn't you wear a sensible outfit when on business? You are showing your pink silk camisole – whatever next!* But John Hibbert didn't seem to notice, concentrating on his driving. He was very skilful and fast – even in these conditions. The Audi sent great bow-waves as we approached Elgin Avenue and my front door. I said:

"Thank you again, John. You were a life-saver."

Again that thin smile. "Just following orders, ma'am." And to my surprise I kissed him on his cheek as I opened the door. I dashed to my own door, then turned to wave as I retrieved my key. But he had gone. Ten minutes later I was soaking in my bath and thinking, *What an odd day this has been, and what a strange man Duncan Maddox is.* Not one's idea of a civil servant at all. But what was his position in the Home Office? Some sort of Customs official? Obviously senior... I had a moment of fantasy perhaps he was a spy master! MI5, or similar. Then I climbed out of the bath – the water was getting cold.

As I dressed in warm clothes, I had another fantasy: by Thursday evening I would be metamorphosed into Aspasia (a famous Athenian courtesan, and Pericles's mistress to those of you who are ignorant of Greek history). Well that, at least, was something to get excited about – let's hope it wasn't raining on the Cote d'Azur.

That evening, having supper with my father, we asked each other, as usual, about our day. I said to him: "Well mine was unusual enough."

"In what way?"

"It was a job for Frances Brook, not the usual tedious document translation. I was working in a Government department – the Home Office, and for this mysterious civil servant."

"Mysterious in which way?"

"Well, first of all he kept me waiting for half an hour, which made me cross..."

My father grinned through his beard. "I can imagine..."

"So I left."

"Oh dear."

"Anyway, I was striding down Marsham Street when he called me on my mobile, and asked me to come back, apologising profusely. He met me at the door, then escorted me to some small, grubby office, where I had to translate a battered paper in Portuguese. Honestly, Dad; it was almost impossible to read. Thank goodness I had the magnifier..."

"No wonder I couldn't find it – why can't you buy your own?"

"Shush, let me finish. Well it took me all day; but what was strange is that there were insertions in Lithuanian – well, as far as I could tell that is what the characters were."

"How very odd. Just a moment, Dawn. Were any of the characters in Cyrillic?"

"I thought you might ask that. To answer your question – no. Things haven't changed very much, have they? Any murky dealings and we automatically ascribe them to the Russians."

"Carry on."

"Anyway, I finished the task in hand, so to speak, while this odd man – Maddox was his name – was in the room. He thanked me – very polite – but when I got outside it was absolutely sheeting down…"

"So I noticed; I was worried about you…"

"So I ran down the street; then this car drew up and Maddox's assistant told me to get in, and he brought me home."

"That was thoughtful."

"Yes; but there was one thing."

"What was that?"

"How did he know where I lived?"

My father poured us the last of the wine. "A simple explanation, is, that Frances supplied that when she confirmed your appointment?"

"Hmmmm."

So I left it at that. Well, not really. Later that evening in bed, I was attempting to read *The Story of Art*, but even Professor Gombrich's elegant prose could not hold me for long. Eventually, I drifted off, and the next thing I knew the morning must have stolen in while I was asleep, and my mobile phone was calling. I spluttered some kind of reply.

"Dawn."

"Yes, what – oh, Dad?"

"Yes: it is now exactly 8.56 a.m. Are you thinking of arising, daughter?"

"What! Oh, God, yes. Thanks Dad."

So I didn't get to the Agency before ten o'clock. "Ah," said Frances, "the wanderer returns. We thought you had been kidnapped by enemy agents, and would now be incarcerated in some horrible East European jail."

"You've been listening too much to your husband, Frances." I sat down in front of her desk.

Frances replied: "I never listen to my husband: that is one of the reasons that we have such a happy marriage. However, that to one side. How did you get on in the corridors of power?"

I gave her a blow-by-blow account of my day. "Good heavens," she said, "it does sound rather cloak and dagger. Anyway, Dawn, thank you for all your efforts."

I spent the rest of the morning in what we call the black hole of Calcutta; which was actually a sound-proof box in the far corner of the building. This is where we transcribe tapes. Everybody hates these jobs; they were the most difficult that the Agency handles. God knew how they get on at the United Nations. Actually, it was not a box: it is was made of glass set into wood panels. Working in there, one feels like being in a fish tank: you can see other people, but can't couldn't hear them.

So I got quite a shock about an hour later when I happened to look up and see someone outside Frances's office. It was the tall brunette I first saw leaving the manager's office at the Quest-Ritson hotel all those weeks ago. She was as stunning as ever, wearing a red silk shirt and black tailored slim skirt; her hair was shorter than I remembered, but brushed back from her forehead. I felt like hiding under the desk – was I being stalked? Or followed by one of Maddox's staff? Then I thought how ridiculous I was being. All this was just a coincidence.

However, about ten minutes' later I (just) heard a knock on the fish tank door. I removed my headphones and looked up: it was Frances. She said, "Come and meet your new colleague." I looked past her; the room was full of my fellow translators (I noticed there were three men and two women; two of the men were staring through Frances's office window).

"What's the matter, Dawn. Are you all right?"

"Sorry, yes – just in the middle of a tricky bit." So I got out of my chair and followed her.

Close up, she didn't seem quite as formidable as when I viewed her from a distance in the Quest-Ritson hotel. Anyhow, she stood and smiled and shook my hand firmly. "Pleased to meet you," she said. "My name's Diana Gilbert. And you are Dawn Hope, yes? Mrs Brooke has explained who you are, and all the languages you understand. You must be very clever."

I didn't know quite what to say after that verbal assault. I wasn't as if Diana Gilbert was being patronising: she just came straight out with it.

Frances just smiled and said: "Look, Diana; Dawn will show you the ropes. Not that there is much to tell." Frances turned to me; by this time, we were sat round Frances's desk, and I thought, *Why me?* Now I was feeling put out. I said:

"Frances: what do you want me to say?"

Frances waved that away. "Oh, I've explained all those details, payment, national insurance, terms of employment – but Diana's going work on a freelance basis. No Dawn: I just thought a friendly chat with you would ease her path."

I could hardly object, but said, "Does that mean lunch *a deux* for Diana and me on the Agency at the Mirabelle?"

"In your dreams."

As it was now 12.30, I left the office with my new companion, and she said, "Where do you usually have lunch – not the Mirabelle, I suppose?"

"Hardly." We wandered down the Strand. "Actually, Diana, I don't usually have lunch – just a sandwich and a cup of coffee."

"If I'm in the City that wouldn't suit me – come on, my treat." I don't know why, but I followed her meekly. Diana Gilbert found one of those bistro-type restaurants in Covent Garden that have the menus written on a blackboard (about ten minutes' walk from the Agency's offices). She slipped her arm through mine, which I found disconcerting, but to her seemed perfectly natural. The familiarity wasn't just off-putting; but I could feel the firmness of her breast against my arm, which made me aware of her sexual vibrations. (Heavens! Was she a lesbian?)

We sat at a corner table just before the lunchtime office crowd invaded. Diana called a waitress over to her before the girl could walk past. She said to me: "What'll we have, Dawn?"

"Anything – I don't mind – nothing too filling?"

Diana smiled at the girl. "We'll have fishcakes, salad, garlic bread and two glasses of *frascati*, please."

I watched this minor performance. I said: "Do you always make sure you get what you want?"

She grinned. "I have a damn good try." She noticed that I was looking at her quizzically. "Something on your mind? Did you think I was rude? Actually, I am not a very nice person, Dawn; in the past I couldn't afford to be."

"I see: well, rather, I don't. Thank you for the advanced warning. I would now describe your attitude as uninhibited candour. Actually, I was just trying to place your accent."

"Were you now… Have a guess. Or isn't my English enunciation good enough?"

The girl brought our meal, and placed a carafe of the white wine on the table.

Diana didn't sound defensive. I said: "No, not at all: perfect. I'll make a guess – East Anglia? Norfolk?"

"Right first time. Well done."

We ate silently for a while. I was intrigued by this young woman. I attempted to start the conversation. I looked at her left hand – the wedding and engagement rings; the four diamonds caught the light. I said: "That is a beautiful engagement ring."

Diana placed her fork on the plate and lifted her hand.

"Isn't it gorgeous? Max popped the question over dinner at the Ivy Restaurant."

"Of course! Max! Mrs Gilbert! You are married to Max Gilbert the bird artist!"

Diana grinned. "That's right: we've been married just over a year."

Then I nearly put my foot in it. "But isn't he…?"

"Older than I? That's right – nearly thirty years. But I love him."

I blushed. "Oops, sorry. Only…"

"You thought, what am I doing being married to an old man? Let me tell you something. Max and I understand each other. I promised that I would always look after him. In return he has given me a safe home in Pimlico and a comfortable existence and freedom of movement. I was an orphan, you see." Diana drained her glass. "I may not be a nice girl, but I am loyal."

"That's quite a confession on such a short acquaintance."

Diana waved her hand; the diamonds flashed again. "So," she said, 'what about you, Dawn Hope?"

"Nothing much to tell. Only child of old-ish parents. My mother died three years ago. I live with my father, a retired professor of linguistics, in Maida Vale. I did a degree in modern languages, then a master's; spent some time Italy."

"Got a man in your life?"

"I will comment on that when I know you better."

Diana laughed. "Which means you have. Is he incredibly rich? Buys you diamonds and fancy underwear?"

I felt myself blushing again. She said:

"You're a lovely-looking lady, Dawn. A natural blonde? I know a few who would die for your complexion."

"My grandparents on my mother's side were Norwegian." Now I was feeling quite uncomfortable, so I said: "Diana?"

"Yes?"

"Stop being so bloody nosy."

She laughed out loud, then called for the bill. I watched her open her purse and pull out a roll of notes. Diana studied the bill. She said to the waitress: "What is this 12½%?"

"Discretionary service charge, madam."

"Then why is it included in the total?"

"I don't know. It is always billed like that." I could see that the girl was looking very uncomfortable. Diana said: "If I want to show my appreciation I will leave a tip. But I don't expect to be pressurised by the management. Take it back and bring a new total, all right?"

The girl scuttled away. It seemed that my new acquaintance had the bad habit of putting people's backs up. As we left the restaurant, I said so, bluntly.

Diana shrugged. "I don't like people trying to rip me off." We both walked briskly across the paving flags of the pedestrian square. Diana headed towards the Tube station; I was going back to the Agency. Then she stopped, and said: "I'll probably be working from home. I don't know whether we'll run across each other again."

"We might. Thanks for the lunch."

She smiled. "*De rien*. Are you a real art lover, Dawn?"

"Very much so."

"Then give me your phone number. Maybe you and your father would like to meet Max?"

"That would be lovely."

We went our separate ways. Well, that had been a memorable meeting. But I wasn't sure that I liked Diana Gilbert very much.

Chapter Four

London, Piccadilly: Royal Academy of Arts

New Dawn? Old Dawn? That was the question. And it was one I had to answer fairly soon – or so I told myself. I had returned from my weekend with Carlo nearly three weeks ago; since then, I had an unwanted feeling of dissatisfaction, of disorientation. Previously, I was sure that the way I led my life – absorbing work, lovely days with Carlo – was complete; I had everything I needed; I was fulfilled.

Oh, and looking at beautiful paintings, which was where I was now, at the R.A.'s Summer Exhibition, with my father sitting beside me. We were staring at a huge abstract, while sipping champagne. My father said:

"An observation, Dawn."

"Yes, Dad."

He nodded towards the painting. "Is that canvas so large, (a), to justify its acceptance as a work of art; (b) because the artist always paints at that size; or (c) to satisfy the artist's ego?"

"Are you saying that it may not be acceptable unless it was huge – in other words, that is its only merit – a great splash of yellows and reds? That it is merely attention seeking – that the artist lacks integrity?"

"That is part of what I am asking."

I smiled. My father and I had played this game many times. I said, "I don't intend to give you any answer you may expect, father, dear: I believe I have replied to all three points. Make up your own mind."

My father laughed; but it sounded to me as if he was dismissing contemporary abstract expressionism; I had the same opinion as he – but I wasn't going to tell him that. I glanced sideways at him: he looked good. He was wearing a lightweight summer suit; a crisp white shirt; a loosely-knotted bow tie. His beard was neatly trimmed; the pain lines under his eyes seemed to be smoothed out. Perhaps this acupuncturist that Anne Holt had found was doing something for him. We stood and moved away through the grand hall. He took my arm. I said, "You OK, Dad?"

"Of course! I am with my daughter and enjoying myself."

This was the first day of the Summer Exhibition; I was a 'Friend' of the R.A., so I had a ticket for us both. Waiters were gliding around with trays of champagne; I returned our flutes; and then – as we moved into the next gallery – I saw a figure in the crush that I thought I knew. I was right. *But of course she would be here.* Standing next to Diana Gilbert was a sharp-featured, dapper man; presumably her husband.

There were about half-a-dozen people looking at a painting with their backs to the Gilberts; the picture was obviously exciting a lot of interest. Diana Gilbert turned her head. "It's you! Dawn!" She moved towards us, her hand holding her husband's elbow. "Darling: this is Dawn Hope. You remember I'd met her and I told you?"

Mr Gilbert gave me a quick appraisal, then looked at my father. He extended his hand, and said: "And you must be Professor Hope." My father seemed amused by this unlikely duo. Diana was looking glamorous in a dark blue chiffon number and a floppy hat; her husband wore a pale-grey suit, a rosebud in his buttonhole.

Anyhow, we all shook hands, then I turned my attention to the painting that had drawn such interest. Max Gilbert grinned mischievously at me, then said, "Ah: so what do you think, Dawn? Have I captured my wife?"

I thought, *You could say that.* It was an astonishing painting. Max Gilbert had made Diana (for it was immediately obvious that it was her) so sexually assertive that it was almost embarrassing. This picture was not a nude or erotic in a pornographic sense. He had shown her stood half-length in three-quarter profile, her head turned to the viewer. She was dressed in a white shirt open almost to her waist, showing her breasts straining against the shirt. Over this she wore a green leather waistcoat. Her black hair was swept back from her forehead, topped with a forage cap; a long feather sprouted from the rim. But the most startling section was her right hand and arm, covered in a gauntlet, held horizontally, for there was a bird of prey with its wicked claws on her fist. Its wings were about to spread and its head – with glinting yellow eyes – looked as if it was about to spring out of the picture and attack the viewer. I thought about my original impression of Diana – trouble. What could I say to Max Gilbert?

"Mr Gilbert: You have two very dangerous characters in that picture. But I think it is wonderful. A falcon, I presume. But it is not hooded?"

Max Gilbert smiled. "Oh, no. Are you alarmed?" He was teasing.

But I glanced at my father (obviously amused) and then to Diana, who gave the same enigmatic smile that was in her picture. I said to Max Gilbert, "Actually, when I first looked, Mr Gilbert, I was reminded of Da Vinci's Lady with an Ermine."

"Max, please. So you are an art historian, Dawn, as well as a linguist?"

"Hardly, Max: just an abiding enthusiast." He turned his attention to my father:

"And you also, Professor?"

"Hardly; but I always accompany Dawn to these artistic shindigs, especially the summer exhibition – it's always such a jolly occasion."

There was further bantering, then we excused ourselves with promises to meet sometime in the near future (does one ever keep these promises – or is it the usual English hypocrisy to get one out of a situation without seeming to be too brusque?). So we completed the tour; then I noticed my father was getting tired, so I took him off to the Friends' room for coffee. He was pensive as we took our time over the refreshments; I didn't think too much of it: for he was a quiet man. Eventually he said:

"What an odd couple they make."

I now knew what he had been thinking. "The Gilberts, Dad?"

"Yes."

I laughed. "I know what you mean: there must be at least twenty-five years between them. Ah, well. But did you enjoy this year's exhibition?" To be truthful, I didn't want to start discussing relations between older and younger couples, for obvious reasons.

When we reached home, I went to my room and checked my emails. No messages from Carlo; none from the translation agency. Nobody. What was Carlo doing at this moment? And where? But tomorrow was Saturday; and I woke to a day that bloomed even warmer than yesterday. I could see across to the park, and notice that the neatly mown grass was turning straw-coloured.

After breakfast, my father went into his study and his beloved stamp collection. I sat on our small terrace at the rear of the house overlooking the narrow garden, reading. For once it was nothing to do with art: I was reading Kate Adie's *From Corsets to Camouflage*, her history of women in wartime. Fancy having a life like Adie's! Dodging bullets all over the world, all in the name of being a journalist. I felt a tinge of envy. Then it made me think of what Hibbert had said when I collared him in Nice; that Maddox was thinking of offering me a job. Job? What sort of job? I got the impression that his was a murky world of smugglers and other criminals. No, thank you. I was satisfied with my life, wasn't I? In fact very fortunate; but I had to admit feeling a frisson of anticipation when I was in Maddox's office, attempting to decipher that nearly incomprehensible sheet of paper. It was not the sort of challenge I had in day-to-day work. Mmmm: what would I say if he contacted me?

I went back to my book. But I didn't read for long: the telephone rang – perhaps as a sign of synchronicity. This was the weekend – Saturday afternoon. What was I thinking? A strike at hope of more excitement? If it was Carlo telling me to get the first plane out of the City Airport ('A car will collect you in one hour') then I would do so. What if it were Maddox, saying, 'We have a national emergency; come at once to Thames House (Security Service HQ), we need you to talk to a woman who has info about a major terrorist plot'? *And when was I going to hear from Carlo?*

Such silly fantasy brought me down to earth by Susan Robinson's sensible voice:

"Dawn – this is Susan."

"Oh, hi, Susan – how are you?"

"I'm actually on my own – and feeling a bit bereft. May I come round later? Bring some grub? We could have a girls' night in?"

"That would be lovely; just what I need, Susan."

"Are you sure. Rather short notice, dear."

"Of course: and don't bring food. We'll have Parma ham and salad and a bottle of Aussie chardonnay. You can't keep feeding half the community's adolescents, Susan. About six?"

I advised my father about this tête-à-tête.

"Then I shall leave you girls to it," he said.

Guiltily, I said, "But I'll bring you some supper, Dad!"

"No, you won't. I'll look after myself."

The above seems a rather convoluted and unnecessary description of a small domestic arrangement, but don't forget that I was a woman, and feeling guilty about seeming neglect of my family rears its head very quickly. Susan Robinson arrived promptly at six and we sat at a white-painted, round, cast-iron table on the terrace. As we sipped our first glass of wine, I studied her. Susan had one of those round clear faces where everything seemed to be in proportion: widely set hazel eyes, a broad brow, and a generous mouth. She smiled a lot. I said:

"So where are all your menfolk?"

"Well Alex is at the gardening club – some lecture on aphids, or something…"

"That sounds enthralling?"

Susan grinned. "Philip is on a dig in Cumbria with his girlfriend. And Jonathan is at Rebecca's parents' place having been invited to supper. I think the Doctors Fairfax are on a guilt trip because I'm always feeding their daughter."

I laughed. "Hence my remark when I spoke to you on the phone."

She frowned at me. "I blame you basketball players – we live far too near the sports hall!"

I always felt comfortable in Susan Robinson' presence; she seemed always so calm, so steady; I bet she instilled all kinds of confidence in her patients. I was mulling this over as we ate our supper, then she placed her knife and fork neatly on her plate, picked up the bottle and refilled our glasses. She said: "Now, Dawn Hope: confession time."

"Pardon?"

Again that grin. "Tell me to mind my own business, but you have been looking very sparky lately with a blush to your cheeks; I've also noticed some very smart clothes. The question is: What's his name?"

With anyone else I would have been annoyed and told them to mind their own business. So I returned her grin, and said, "Well, there is someone I see when I'm working in Europe, but you know how it is, Susan: we both have busy lives. I might be in Barcelona; he could be in Milan. But we do manage to spend some time together. The arrangement seems to work OK most of the time." I hoped that sounded sufficiently glib to halt any further questions. All she said after that was:

"Well he must think the sun shines out of you: Jonathan was drooling over the Merc that collected you last week. Has he got enormous amounts of dosh?"

I changed tack. "And who is that frizzy-haired, kooky-looking girl who follows Jonathan around? I know she's a good basketball player…"

Susan laughed. "Rebecca Fairfax? The doctors' daughter? Jonathan keeps saying she's a pest and he doesn't like her. But that doesn't seem to stop her – poor boy doesn't get a word in edgeways."

We continued our chatter along those lines. Then Susan asked about my father. "I hope the new medication is satisfactory?"

A voice behind us: "Very well indeed, Susan," said my father. "Am I allowed in? Did I tell you about my acupuncture regime?" And he pulled up a chair and helped himself to the last of our wine. He continued: "Did you know that acupuncture has been used as a pain relief in China for the last one thousand years?"

We sat silently and politely while he gave us a ten-minute lecture on Chinese medicine…

Susan Robinson walked into the bedroom wearing a brightly coloured towel wound round her head. Her husband – propped up on pillows and reading Amateur Gardening – looked up, stared at his wife and said:

"You look like the Queen of Sheba."

Susan sat on the edge of the duvet and replied, "Pardon?"

"The towel, darling; all the exotic colours, contrasting with the whiteness of your – rather short – bath robe."

"Why Sheba?"

"Because there is also something biblical about your ensemble."

"What were you drinking at the gardening club?"

"Tea, Susan. By the way, when you sat on the bed and crossed your legs, I saw all the way up your thigh."

"Well, bully for you, Alex Robinson: some people have all the luck. By the way, would you like to hear a titbit of gossip?"

"Not particularly."

"Shhh – pay attention. Dawn has an admirer."

"What a charmingly old-fashioned phrase. But it is hardly surprising; she is a good-looking girl, very intelligent. But I always felt that she might put men off."

"Really?" His wife sounded surprised that her husband should show such perception. "Anyway, I think he is a wealthy business man who flits around Europe in a private jet, and is having this torrid affair with our neighbour, showering her with diamonds and designer clothes."

Her husband quickly lost interest in all this and returned to his magazine, and Susan continued filing her finger nails, a bit put out that Alex ignored her gossip.

When she finished that important task, she slipped off her robe and slid under the duvet next to her husband. He put down his magazine. "Susan, you are in the nude."

"Yes. Been awfully warm today, don't you think? Do you want to switch off the bedside light?"

"What, now?"

"Yes, please."

Chapter Five

Strand: London

I had a strong feeling that my question to myself would be taken out of my hands – *Quo Vadis*?

I woke to a working day; a Monday morning, the sun streaming through my bedroom windows, making outlandish patterns on the carpet. Dutifully, I left my bed as the alarm on the bedside table buzzed. I showered, made up my face in a subdued manner, dressed for the office (white blouson, light-grey trouser suit), and collected my business valise.

Breakfasting with my father was a silent ritual: we didn't speak until the second cup of tea. Then I said: "See you tonight, Dad?"

"Indeed you will, Dawn. Take care. Yes?"

"Of course." I kissed his cheek.

Frances wasn't at the agency offices when I strolled in at 9 o'clock – neither could I see any of my colleagues. But Harry, Frances's husband was. I stuck my head round his door. He glanced at my right hand. I said:

"Have all the birds flown the nest?"

He looked over his glasses at me. Harry was ploughing through account and expenses sheets; the printer at the PC was going full blast. He replied:

"Frances will be back after lunch, for which I am grateful this morning."

"I see. I'd better leave you to it."

"Thank you. Anything else I can do for you?"

"Nothing. Just saying hello."

"Hello and goodbye."

Frances had left some papers on my desk – and a sealed envelope, which I opened immediately. It said:

It seems that Mr Maddox at the Home Office was impressed by your forensic skills. He would like your assistance with another project. Could you please contact him – his direct line phone number is enclosed.

By the way, Dawn, thank you for enhancing the Agency's reputation.

Frances.

Praise from my boss; that was a first; 'forensic', indeed. There was something fairly sinister about the phrase, but I wondered whether she knew anything at all about my contretemps with Hibbert. First of all, I made a cup of coffee, and then tried to gather my thoughts. When one works freelance, one should try to keep one's options open. So I thought about Commander Maddox for some time then picked up the phone. But he wasn't in. Where was everyone this Monday morning? But I was speaking to a male voice, so I said:

"Is that John Hibbert? This is Dawn Hope. I was asked to call."

"This is Inspector Hibbert," he said rather defensively.

"Well, well; inspector is it, now?"

"I have been an inspector for a month, Miss Hope." He still sounded rather huffy.

"How is it, Inspector, that every time I try to contact your boss he's never there?"

"Commander Maddox is a very busy person."

"So am I." And I put the phone down. Poor Hibbert; he always seems to get the backlash. I spent the morning with hum-drum-this-work-pays-the-bills translations. Just before midday the phone rang. It was my father. "Dawn: I won't be here when you get home; I'm having dinner with Anne Holt. Do you mind coming home to an empty house?"

"Of course not, Dad. Have a nice evening." Sod it; nobody wanted me today. I felt miffed.

Boo-hoo, Dawn. Then I looked out of the office window; a lovely day. Then my mobile phone rang again.

"Miss Hope? Duncan Maddox here."

"Commander! Well, well, what can I do for you?"

"Are you free at lunchtime?"

"Yes."

"Then if you have no other plans could you meet me at St Mary-le-Strand? Perhaps we may talk over lunch. You know St Mary?"

"Of course."

"Twelve-thirty, then. Goodbye."

Actually, I didn't arrive at the rendezvous with Maddox until twelve-forty-five (acting like a spoiled brat). But he was there; he even raised his hat when he saw me. But what a strange place for a rendezvous. He carried a bulky briefcase in his left hand. As I approached, he said, "Good afternoon, Miss Hope. Thank you for coming." I stared up at the towers of the church; it always reminded of a rather splendid wedding cake. Maddox caught me looking.

"Are you impressed by the architecture?"

"A bit too much baroque revival for my taste."

We moved into the church; Maddox seemed to know his way around. It was cool and quiet, for which I was grateful after the sweat of the Strand. We skirted the altar and walked through a door in the rear of the building, which led us outside. Much to my surprise, there was a small garden with a bench under a plane tree. Maddox said:

"Shall we sit here?"

Then he opened the case and withdrew a lunch box and a thermos flask. "Chicken or ham?"

"Oh, er, ham, thanks." And he poured us both a cold drink of apple juice.

Then said: "Lovely and peaceful here, don't you think? I often come at lunchtime."

"Very nice – but what does the vicar say?"

Maddox smiled. "He's an old friend. By the way, did you know that this church is connected with the Wrens?"

I mustn't have heard him right for I said, "It wasn't designed by Christopher Wren!"

"No, no: the connection is with the Women's Royal Naval Service – the WRNS."

Sitting in this quiet church garden, it was difficult to believe that the hub of a great city was minutes away; somehow unreal.

I said, after we had finished Maddox's sandwiches, "Well, that was very nice, Commander. Thank you for lunch. Now, first of all, you can explain why you sent John Hibbert to spy on me. And second, what do you want? According to John Hibbert there was some mention about offering me position? Why would you do that? I have a job."

Maddox folded the wrapping paper from our sandwiches neatly, returned it to his bag, then withdrew that day's copy of The Times. He opened it at page 3. He said, "Is that lady any relation?"

The story concerned the Government's Committee on the Future of Higher Education. "Yes," I replied, "she's my aunt – my father's sister, Lady Margaret Hope, as she now is." There was a profile photograph of Margaret in her baroness's robes, looking severe and distinguished.

Maddox smiled. "She looks formidable."

"She can be. But can we get back to why I am lunching in a churchyard. What was Inspector Hibbert up to – following me around the Cote d'Azur? What do you want from me, Mr Maddox?"

"Well, after you did that little job for me I wanted to see you on an ordinary working day in a European country…"

A likely story!

"So, I had you followed – sorry about that – and Hibbert found himself at Heathrow, wondering what to do next. He showed his ID to the check-in at BA and followed you to Nice and to the Negresco Hotel." Maddox paused and thought for a moment. He turned to me. "I must say, Miss Hope, your employers put you up at some grand hotels."

I shrugged. "It all goes through the client's expense sheet. I didn't particularly like it – it's like staying in a high-class Paris brothel." Maddox didn't enquire how I knew about Paris brothels.

He continued: "And then, of course, he lost you."

I laughed. "Yes he did, and made him look a fool – serves him right. He should think himself lucky I didn't report him to the steward: now that would have been embarrassing, an English detective inspector being arrested by a gendarme."

"Quite. Let us forget that – actually, what he said was, he considered you to be a bossy cow – those were his actual words. But he quite likes you, strange as it may seem."

"Does he now. But let's move on to the second question. Before that: who are you, Mr Maddox, and what is your position?"

Maddox looked over his shoulder, as if finding someone hiding behind the plane tree. "My official title is liaison officer seconded from the Metropolitan Police between the Inland Revenue and Customs, the Special Branch, and the Border Agency. What I am offering you, Dawn, is attachment to my unit as translator, linguist, and investigator. This means that you would not be a member of the permanent staff; but called on when the need arises. Does that appeal to you? It would not affect the other work at your Agency."

"I see. Well that all seems very interesting. First off, you realise that there is a difference between a linguist and a translator?"

Maddox smiled. "But you are both, Miss Hope."

"Quite. So I would be a sort of one-woman quango? I don't wish to sound too avaricious, Commander – but what's in it for me? Can the Civil Service match my earnings and expenses? I can hardly imagine them sanctioning my being put up at the Negresco." (Actually, I loathe the vulgar Negresco. I would have to have a word with Carlo about our accommodation in future rendezvous.)

"Hardly."

"If I do find myself interested in your intriguing offer, Commander, I assume that there would be a formal letter, etc.? Conditions of employment and remuneration?"

"Of course – expect to hear from my office within the next seven days. If you accept, there will be a period of induction and orientation, and also it will be necessary for you to sign the Official Secrets Act, which puts you under a legal obligation. Do you understand?"

I thought, *But what do 'induction' and 'orientation' (horrible word) mean?*

"I believe so – will I be a spook and get to meet 007?"

Maddox frowned. "And I would advise you to curb your infantile sense of humour." What could he mean? However, we went our separate ways, and I returned to the Agency offices.

Frances beckoned me as I entered. She said: "Did you get my note, Dawn?"

"I did and acted on it. I met your pal in a churchyard – which seemed appropriate, somehow."

Frances said: "I hope you weren't too flippant and remembered your manners."

"Moi? I'm a very well brought up girl, Frances. He's obviously an important client. We shared his sandwiches and thermos. He propositioned me."

"I beg your pardon?"

I giggled. "Mr Maddox offered me a part-time position on his staff; a sort of tame linguist-cum-detective, or whatever he calls it. I said I'd think it over once he sent me a formal offer of employment. So what do you think?"

Frances gave me one of her old-fashioned looks. "I don't think anything, Dawn. I only hope he knows what he's doing."

Honestly, you can't please some people: I get full marks for the first job; then a doubtful vote for what could be a permanent position. I'd had enough of the city, so I took work home with me and sat outside the French windows, translated and drank fruit juice. I thought my father would be home at that hour, but he had already left.

I hadn't sat for long when I had a visitor – Hodge, the fat lazy tabby from next door. He sat and looked at me in that disapproving way that spoiled cats do. "And what do you want, Hodge? Whatever it is, I ain't got any, so clear off." He ignored that and spread himself in the afternoon sun on the step.

When I moved back inside the house, I found a note from our 'daily', Mrs Mills, saying she would be here again on Thursday and thanking me for the money I'd left (the place smelled of disinfectant and furniture polish); and one from my father, saying that he was dining in college with Anne ('and two or three anthropologists, who might confirm Darwin's theories by their behaviour'). *Very funny, Dad.* Seriously, though, the idea that I would be certain of future employment with a branch of the Civil Service in these uncertain times was not to be sniffed at.

I finished the batch of work, then felt at a loose end. What about basketball practice? No. Not on a Monday. Then I did the obvious; I phoned Carlo at his HQ. Not there, and some snooty girl wouldn't give any further information. Then his private number. No answer. Lastly, his mobile number – and I got through.

"*Prego.*"

"Carlo! Dawn. Where the hell have you been – I feel terribly neglected."

Silence for a moment. "Darling: I am sorry. Yes, I have been so busy... But I will send you an email this evening, and we will meet. Now I have to go. *Ciao, cara.*"

Well, that was not very satisfactory, Carlo Palladio. But I would just have to wait. It was a lovely evening, so I changed into a track suit and running shoes and jogged round the park a few times to get a sweat on and release any boredom. At home again, I took a shower and washed my hair, then sprayed on some nice lotion, and donned a cotton dress. That did the trick. I was now hungry, so I placed a ready meal in the microwave and while I waited for that, sat on the patio with a glass of chardonnay. Carlo's email, when it arrived, was intriguing:

Miss Hope: thank you for your telephone call. I can assure you that your request is receiving my immediate attention. Watch and wait, please.

So what the hell did that mean? I could understand that he wanted to be discreet; even so I suspected that Italian men had that irresponsible streak in them, but I didn't have to wait long, for next morning I got a telephone call from him at 7.30.

"Where are you, Dawn?"

"In bed."

"Shh."

"What does that mean, *caro*?"

"What are you wearing?"

"Chanel Number 5"

Laughter down the line. "But you are not Marilyn Monroe."

"Where are you?"

"London."

"WHAT?! When did you get into London?"

"Last evening."

"I hate you! Why didn't you say so?"

"It was late."

"Where are you speaking from?"

"The Quest-Ritson Hotel."

"When do I see you?"

"At midday. I will send a car."

"No you won't. I shall be working all morning at my office."

"Do not be late."

"I shall be there when I can. I still hate you."

"Of course you do. *Ciao*."

I was being bloody-minded, of course; and people who are continually bloody-minded usually end up with egg on their face. I left the Tube at Trafalgar Square and made my way up the Strand, leaving the tourists feeding the fat, greedy, stupid pigeons. The day had begun cooler and I could see a few threatening clouds forming behind the National Gallery: this time I was carrying a folding umbrella in my overnight bag. I didn't intend to put myself in the embarrassing position when John Hibbert rescued me last time there was a summer shower.

When I got to the Agency, the air conditioning was switched to 'medium', for which I and my colleagues were grateful; the room was full this morning; I mouthed a 'Good morning' to two people. As I passed her office Frances beckoned to me. She said:

"Do you have…?" She pointed to my document case. I unzipped it and passed them over. "All done?"

"Yes, Frances: all done, plus two copies."

"You look elegant again this morning."

"Thank you."

"Going anywhere special at lunchtime?"

"No. But I'm leaving for Outer Mongolia this evening – rush job for MI5."

"Very amusing. They eat yak fat out there; that won't suit your gourmet's tummy."

"You'd be surprised what suits me."

"I doubt it. By the way, how's your father, Dawn?"

"He's been pretty good lately He's got a lady friend."

Frances looked up from her desk. "Has he now. I assume both your remarks are related?"

"I suppose."

"None of my business, but how do you feel about it?"

Why do people who say that mean exactly the opposite?

"That's fine by me, Frances. If their friendship makes him happy – well, OK. Good luck to him." What else could I say? Any further remark would make me sound like a jealous, possessive daughter... Hmmm. Not so sure about that. But I put it out of my mind and tried to look as if I was clearing my desk, just to keep Frances happy; as it happened, there was very little for me to do, so I left the office and decided to walk slowly to my assignation with Carlo.

I spent half an hour in the National Portrait Gallery, and drank a cup of green tea in their cafe, wondering about my future. I was still pondering when I continued my journey down Piccadilly to Sloane Ranger land and the Quest-Ritson hotel. As I entered the foyer, the concierge offered to take my grip-bag; I thanked him, but held on to my document case. I hadn't been in the hotel since my previous meeting all those weeks ago. But it had not altered (why should it?); the same quiet, discreet decor; the flowers in the tall Murano vases; a faint scent that hung in the air. The young woman receptionist looked up as I approached. She said:

"Good morning. How may I help you?" With a brilliant smile.

"Mr Palladio is expecting me. Dawn Hope?"

"Of course, Miss Hope. Signor Palladio asked me to tell you he would be in the garden restaurant." I nodded and thanked her. Very smooth and efficient. I walked into the restaurant, looking for my lover. As one moves into this pretty room it is necessary to turn sharp left; consequently, one has a distorted view (through the glass door) of the hotel lobby. As I looked, I stopped and saw a woman emerging from the manager's office with the manager; she was laughing and he looked rather uncomfortable. He stood still, his hands behind his back, while she held on to his elbow; then she patted his cheek, turned on her heel and waved goodbye, still laughing.

It was Diana Gilbert. Now what was she doing here? Well, well…

A voice whispering in my ear: "On whom are you spying, my love?" Carlo was behind me; he slipped his hand round my waist and gently touched my breast.

I blushed and turned, saying, "One does not grope young ladies in this sort of high-class establishment, signore…"

I hugged him and kissed him. We sat at a table overlooking the garden; there was a small bowl of sweet peas between us, and their scent seemed overpowering. I felt dizzy; so I took a long, slow deep breath. Carlo took my hand. *God*, I thought, *Carlo, you are too handsome, too elegant, too wealthy, too charming…* And I suddenly felt very hungry. He lifted a frosted bottle out of the ice bucket, and poured champagne. We touched glasses. He said:

"Do you still hate me, *cara*?"

The wine was glorious. *Oh, Carlo, Carlo… Of course I do: I also adore you: and I love you and where have you been?* He was dressed in a cream suit, pale blue shirt with red silk tie, and shiny brown loafers: and I could have gobbled him up there and then. Carlo said, "Are you hungry?"

"Yes: very."

"Then I shall attend to all your needs."

Carlo watched me munch my way through warm quiche lorraine and green salad, then salmon and mayonnaise; he seemed to eat very little, just the salmon with a green salad. And to make sure I didn't become hungry before dinner I ate a crème brûlée. All through the lunch I felt him watching me; he seemed amused. As I pushed the dessert plate away, he said:

"Dawn, it has occurred to me whom you would be – how do I say? – ah, yes. A Nordic goddess. A female warrior with yellow hair."

"Very flattering, I am sure. How very Wagnerian – or should I be in the lair of the mountain king? You have been listening to too much opera, Don Palladio."

He laughed at that, then leant across the table. 'What shall we do now, *cara*?"

"Need you ask?"

I woke, and the sun was still dispersing through the long net curtains. A gentle breeze moved them across the long windows. I turned in the bed: Carlo wasn't there. I slipped out of bed, donned my silk kimono and looked in the bathroom: nobody there. Then I found a note on the bedside table. It said: '*When you wake, join me in Park Gardens, Mayfair. I have something to show you. The concierge will guide you. CP.*'

So he abandons me after he had had his wicked way with me (or was it the other way around?) then writes me a mysterious note, directing me to another rendezvous. I dressed quickly. And also thought it wise to clear the debris of our lovemaking – such as my dress and underwear scattered on the carpet; also, I had to hang his suit in the wardrobe; and place his shirt in the laundry and dump evidence in the bathroom trash can. God, men really are useless. What on earth was he up to now? And why Mayfair?

So I eventually found myself strolling down towards Belgrave Square, past the U.S. Embassy (Carlo, carelessly, hadn't given me a proper address – Men, honestly…) after finding 'Park Gardens' on the internet. Which wasn't a garden, but an apartment block, and not really Mayfair at all. I wondered if his secretary found him as irritating?

Park Gardens was obviously a newly-refurbished slice of London Regency real estate. There were tall, shiny black cast-iron railings all round the building; they led in a curved manner at the side of the steps to the entrance. I also noticed (from my position across the street) that the developers had retained the outer facade of the development; the Royal Borough and Estates would have had something to say about that! There were newly planted London plane trees precisely two metres apart in the pavement outside. On the ground-floor windows they had placed window-boxes with the inevitable red geraniums. Looking closely from my position, I noticed CCTV cameras dotted discreetly all over the walls. I dodged the traffic and found myself against heavy, polished oak doors; to my right was a long series of numbered buttons, like a pearly king's hat. I pressed one that said Concierge.

"Yes?" He didn't sound particularly welcoming.

"Good afternoon to you. Dawn Hope. Mr Palladio is expecting me."

"One moment."

I stood on this elegant doorstep impatiently; eventually there was a buzz and the double glass door slid open. I strode inside, fuming. The concierge stood behind a polished walnut desk; it was in the corner of a wide lobby; my heels clicked noisily on the marble floor. The space was lit by two faux empire chandeliers. There was a lift at the end of the lobby facing me. He picked up a phone as I stood there, replaced it, and said:

"Signor Palladio is on his way."

I'm going to sort you, I thought. At that moment, Carlo emerged from the lift, accompanied by another man. I said to the concierge: "How long have you worked here?"

"Er, one month."

"Well let me tell you something. When somebody rings your buzzer, you reply, 'Good afternoon. How may I help you'. Understand? And also the magic words 'please' and 'thank you' do not go amiss. Have you got that?"

"Er, yes, madam. I'm sorry…"

"Good. Now I suggest you get lost and think about what I've said. I've got private business with Mr Palladio." He vanished. Carlo looked puzzled; his companion embarrassed. Carlo had changed into a dark blue suit with white shirt and subdued neck-tie. He introduced me to his companion. "Maurice, meet my personal assistant, Dawn Hope."

"Dawn: this is Maurice Osbaldiston, the manager here."

Osbaldiston and I were formally polite. I said to Carlo, in Italian (now I was being rather rude, of course):

"Carlo, what the hell is this place – a bordello?"

"Behave, my sweet. On this occasion you are my secretary. I have injected a lot of investment into this building. All the apartments are sold except one. That is ours."

I was too surprised to say anything. Anyway, I stood back while those two talked technicalities. While this was going on I looked around at the entrance to the apartments. Luxurious was hardly an accurate description – the floor was of black and white marble; in the centre was a star-shaped logo with the initials 'PG' (presumably Park Gardens) in red and gold terrazzo. The walls were covered in figured red damask. Light sconces (also in gold) were set in the walls with triple bulbs under silk shades. On either side of the lift doors were two canvases in ornate gilt frames under green wall lights. Or rather, reproductions that I recognised immediately – J.M.W. Turner's *Venus and Adonis* (which seemed appropriate for this setting) and a John Constable, *The Opening of Waterloo Bridge* (at least I hoped they were reproductions, or the Trustees of the Tate might have something to say about it). Myself, I wouldn't have chosen the Constable – an Alma-Tadema, perhaps.

Carlo and I entered the lift, which moved us swiftly and smoothly to the top floor – the sixth. So it was hardly a skyscraper. I followed Carlo as he strode down the carpeted hallway. It sank under our feet. It was very quiet. The walls were covered in the same figured red damask, and further reproductions in gilt frames were under green shades. I played a mental game to see whether I recognised the pictures. We turned a corner and Carlo halted at double metal doors, which he then unlocked. We walked into diffused daylight: a long high window draped fine net; it covered the whole length of one side of the apartment. I was fearfully expecting the rooms to be replicas of the incredible vulgarity of the entrance to the block and its corridors. But the rooms – living-room, two bedrooms, kitchen, and bathroom utility – were what I can only describe as 'Italian minimalist'. In other words, spacious, with avant-garde furniture, furnishings, and wall hangings. It looked as though it had been put together by the chief designer at Maserati.

I stood rooted, not sure whether I liked it; working out in my mind the reasons for not liking the place. First, I did not approve of Carlo springing surprises on me. Second, whether I could live in such a soulless place. I threw my shoulder bag on to a cream leather sofa. Carlo said, "Well, Dawn, what do you think of it. Eh? Just look at the view across London! And what a situation for a London apartment, si?' He spread his arms in a munificent gesture and gave me broad grin.

I said: "Very nice, Carlo. Now please tell me what is going on."

"Going on? What do you mean? This beautiful apartment is just for us!"

"Really, well this is the first I've heard of it, Carlo. What's the game? You leave a mysterious note, telling to meet you at an address unknown to me. And when I arrive you drag me to a top of a building, then tell me this is our apartment."

"But, darling, I wanted to surprise you!"

"Well I don't like surprises, Carlo; and neither do I like assumptions. What am I supposed to do with this enormous, obviously very expensive apartment when you are not here? Come in twice a week and clean it; open the windows to let some air in; collect the bills? And perhaps just sit here and dream of you – Carlo: what did you think you were doing? If you remember, we have been here before." Carlo stared at me, frowning, not understanding what I had just said – or rather, not understanding why I had said it.

"Dawn! You do not like the apartment? You are concerned about the expense? But it is paid for! I own half the building! You have no worries." He shrugged. "You or I use it whenever we like."

He still did not understand where I was coming from. "No, Carlo: I do not like the apartment. When will you learn not to take it for granted that I will always fall in with your wishes?"

"I am sorry, Dawn! But you see, I needed a base for my new operations in London. I cannot continually stay in hotels; privacy and security are important. I have all the latest IT connections here. So, instead of having just an office in the City this situation is ideal. Yes?"

I had calmed down by the time Carlo had finished; and of course what he said seemed reasonable. I thought: *Dawn Hope, you knew what you were taking on when you got involved with him, and we both knew what it would be like, didn't we? You are just pissed off because he didn't tell you what was happening – so stop the sulk and stop behaving like a spoiled brat.*

And as I looked at him, so confident so charming, I ran across the carpet and hugged him, and said I was sorry too, and loved him very much – all the soppy stuff. *God, Dawn; you can be a pain in the bum at times.* As I emerged from the lift and entered the ground floor lobby (after arranging to meet Carlo for dinner later that evening) the general manager, Mr Osbaldiston, dark-suited and showing plenty of white cuff from his jacket sleeves, approached me and said:

"Miss Hope, I hope that the concierge didn't upset you too much."

"Hardly, Mr Osbaldiston. Perhaps I was bit over-reactive. I didn't want to upset anyone." Osbaldiston seemed uncomfortable, almost nervous. He said:

"Only one has to be… if you take my meaning."

"Because your concierge is black? I would have said the same if he had been white. If it makes you feel better, tell him that I'm not such a dragon. OK?"

"Of course, and thank you."

So that was all right, then. What a lot of fuss over nothing.

Chapter Six

Maida Vale

After my bizarre meeting with Carlo I was home, with my father, drinking wine with our evening meal. I looked at him: he seemed distracted; or perhaps just thoughtful; after all, I had arrived late last evening; I had managed only to knock on his bedroom door (he had left the landing light on) and stick my head round. He was propped in bed, reading.

"Everything OK, Dad?"

"Yes: but more to the point, how are you?"

"Absolutely fine. No problems. What are you reading; *Decline and Fall?*"

"Why on earth would I want to read that? No. *Birds of the North Norfolk Coast.*"

"Max Gilbert?"

"Yes. You left it in the study."

I picked up that morning's copy of The Times. There was an interview with my Aunt Margaret, concerning her committee's preliminary report on the future of higher education. I said:

"Have you read this, Dad?"

"The interview with Margaret? Indeed I have." He laughed.

"She says, in effect, that undergraduate education would be improved when – and only when – adolescents entering college could prove that they (a) were numerate and (b) could demonstrate that they could construct a sentence and spell the words correctly. At one time one could be confident that that would be done."

My father laughed again and said, "That won't endear her to the secondary school teachers."

"Aunt Margaret won't think that is funny; privately, Dad, she considers that they – primary and secondary –are not up to scratch. What do you think?"

He looked at me. "I don't, Dawn. I have no interest in the failings or otherwise of the teaching profession. But I am interested in whether you will be assisting me on the Codex tomorrow. Hmmm?"

So that was the end of that conversation. I thought, *Ah that could be a sign of age: a man in his early seventies would think that he would not waste his time on something in which he was not involved.* His revision on the Commentary to the Codex seemed to have given him a new lease of life (but of course Anne Holt had something to do with that). It is said that youth's impatience is always apparent; but I had noticed that the elderly had the same attitude – time's a stuff age will not endure... if you will excuse the mixed metaphor. I said: "Dad: I'll be in my room if you want me. OK?"

He smiled at me and replied: "Of course, darling girl o' mine. And thank you." As I was leaving, he said, "You know, Dawn, you do remind me of your Scandinavian grandmother at times."

I gave him a look and went to my room. What was that supposed to mean? Was he getting weird? Ironic? Sardonic? I needed to think: so one of my methods was distraction. Hardly helpful? It was to me. However, to those readers who would not approve/dislike a description of a young woman naked, dripping with expensive suds, then displaying herself in a long mirror in her lingerie, followed by descriptions of her Italian designer dresses – please turn the page. On second thoughts I won't go into that at all. But I did have a long bath and washed my hair, finishing up in my chaste bed, wrapped in a warm gown, with a mug of cocoa, and a book.

But Professor Gombrich didn't hold my interest for long (my failing, not the author's). I looked at the photograph on my little Chinese cabinet: me and Carlo, taken in Cap Ferrat. I sighed, turned over and went to sleep.

***

Let me go back to how I got involved with all that.

Well, I could say it happened just like this; and move immediately on to how I was recruited. But no: It was more a feeling of dissatisfaction at the time that had crept up on me; a sense of ennui. Put shortly, I was getting fed up with running around Europe, dropping everything at a moment's notice to trail behind some businessman. Like so many decisions we make, we assume that the result would be clear; in other words, it would be a straight case of cause and effect. So I said to myself, I will tell Frances that my Agency work for her would not involve my leaving the country; all my translations for her would be documentary and in London. Whether she would accept that – well, I should have to see. I was even prepared to do Court translation work. Meanwhile, my father wanted my assistance on the Codex; although how I could be of any use with dead languages, God only knew.

But the following morning my father did find a use for me. He had started on revising his Commentary and scribbling notes on his PC (only my father would use his PC as a scribbling pad). So I was the lowly proof reader as he printed out the sheets. I knew that I would have to do this tedious task three or four times (why did I volunteer?). Even so, I welcomed it, I was home, with my father, and we worked to a regular but not onerous routine: starting at 9 a.m., broke for coffee at 11 a.m., worked until 12:45. We would then have lunch, after which Dad would rest for an hour, and I would slump on the sofa and read. We would work for another couple of hours in the afternoon – or even less if we felt like it. Our routine was interrupted half way through the week by a telephone call. To my surprise, it was Diana Gilbert.

"Hello, Dawn! Guess who?"

"Hi, Diana. And what can I do for you?" I realised that I sounded terse, and expected a sharp reply. But she replied:

"It's what I can do for you – if you accept my invitation?"

"Oh, I see…"

She laughed. "Max and I would like the pleasure of your company at dinner – are you both free this Friday evening?" Diana had wrong-footed me, but I put the phone down and checked with my father, who said,

"With Max Gilbert? I should be delighted!"

I said to Diana, "We'd love to: your husband has made a hit with my dad; it must be that copy of Birds of the Norfolk Coast."

"Seven on Friday, then? Look forward to it."

I said, "It is now five minutes to eleven, Dad. Are you going to make the coffee? And there are sponge buns in a biscuit tin on the kitchen shelf."

"Mmm. Do you think I am capable, Dawn: an old man like me?"

"Father: that ploy no longer works. If you don't do as I say, I will tell Dr Anne Holt how useless you are."

In mock alarm, he said: "You wouldn't dare!"

"Try me. By the way, where is she?"

He stood with the help of his stick. In a huff, he said, "I shan't tell you." He walked stiffly towards the kitchen, and I followed him.

I said: "I wonder whether Cambridge will enjoy her lectures?"

"It's not Cambridge, it's Edinb... You are a very naughty girl!"

Why do fathers persist in thinking that they can outwit their daughters? But we sat amicably over our coffee.

After I cleared the cups and plates and returned to the study, I said: "Dad: I've decided to make a change in my working." He looked up from the photographic copy of the palimpsest.

"Really, in which direction?"

"I'm tired of running around Europe, being nice to everyone at business conferences, and socialising in the evening with people I don't wish to know. I want to stay in England – London, preferably."

Dad put down his magnifier. "Have you told Frances?"

"Not yet. I'll go into the office tomorrow. I'd even do Court translation work..."

"You didn't like that very much, complaining about the pay, and being kept hanging around for hours."

"I know, I know. But I can't have everything. Actually, there may be a new opening elsewhere in the government."

"Really: in what capacity? I can't imagine you being a civil servant."

"Quite. Do you remember that job for that man called Maddox? He's some sort of secret cop – I could never make out whether he was attached to the Revenue and Customs or police Special Branch."

"Good lord: it all sounds fearfully hush-hush."

I grinned. "How about that, Pop? Dawn, the female 007, dressed in tight black leather with a knife tucked in my trousers and a pistol in my cleavage?"

"Shall we get back to work?"

I wondered what Frances would say to my plan; but as it happened, she didn't seem surprised when I called the following morning. I sat opposite her in her office. She said, "As it happened, your timing may be right, Dawn."

"Really, how's that?"

"You will no doubt recall the job for the Home Office or Customs, or whatever it was?"

"I'm not likely to forget the job or Mr Maddox."

"Quite. Well it seems that you were more than a little adequate, and they may want to employ you again."

"How kind. I love it when Government departments want to do me favours."

"If I were you I would curb the sarcasm. The Home Office has a limited sense of humour."

"Well, it usually means that I lose out along the line."

"Leave me, rebellious child. Await my instructions."

I got back home by lunch time; my father had made sandwiches, and we ate them in the kitchen. He said, "Anything to report?"

"It seems that all is well in the State of Denmark." My father smiled (this was a family joke). "And the mysterious Commander Maddox requires my services again on a fairly regular basis. It should be interesting."

"Would you have the ambiguous title of 'Consultant'? This government seems to go in for that."

"I don't know. I have yet to hear the details."

After that, I put the matter out of my mind and we finished the week on my father's work. Come Friday, I was looking forward to the evening with the Gilberts. Which, as it turned out, was most enjoyable – except for a small bombshell presented to me by Diana (I'll come to that shortly).

My father said, "You'll have to remind me where we change on the Tube for Pimlico."

"We're not going by Tube; we're going to be extravagant and take a taxi."

So we climbed into a cab at 6.30 that evening. My father wore a dark suit and a maroon bowtie; I wore a 'little black dress' (memories of Venice so long ago!). In his left hand, Dad held a bunch of spring flowers for our hostess. The taxi dropped us a couple of yards from the Gilberts' front door; this gave us an opportunity to weigh up the building as we approached.

It was in a narrow terrace, at least three storeys high. It was double fronted; one attained the front door by three short steps. The door was painted a deep glossy green; there was a shiny brass knocker in the shape of a gannet's head. I knocked, and the door was opened almost instantly, and Diana faced us. She wore a dark green silk dress the same colour as her front door, so when she opened it she appeared like a jack-in-the-box.

"You're here! Everything all right? Good. Edgar, what lovely flowers!" She led us into the lobby, kissing my father, then me. The tiled lobby led onto a double further door, set in coloured panes in an intricate art-nouveau design. "Max is in the drawing room, pouring drinks – champers if we're lucky." I was amused: Diana was obviously the chatelaine; one knew immediately who was in charge of this domestic set-up.

Max rose from a leather, button-back chair as we entered and shook our hands-and also kissing me on the cheek. Diana demonstrated her hostess role by handing round hors-d'oeuvres while we were sipping champagne; Max Gilbert beaming at his wife, proud that this beautiful woman was such a sparkling hostess. I felt a pang of envy as I accepted one of the titbits from the silver salver. "That's poached salmon," she said; "the rest is bits of pâté and other rubbish on damp toast." It was no such thing, of course; they were delicious. I felt Max watching me, then he said:

"Well, Dawn, it is good that we all meet together again like this. Edgar, is your glass empty?"

My father said, "I only ever have one glass of champagne before dinner, Max."

Max nodded. "Quite right; it's only the young persons who can take two. Dawn?"

"I'm fine, thank you."

Diana interjected. "We're having just two courses: I think starters are rather a waste of time after champers and bits of nonsense."

Her husband said: "See how she rules us with a rod of iron?" He led us into the dining-room, holding on to my arm, followed by my father. Max whispered to me,

"You are a lovely companion and you smell delightful, Miss Hope."

"Behave, Max: how much champagne have you had?" He laughed and pulled out my chair. This old-fashioned dinner party set-up continued by Max sitting at the head of the long (highly polished) dining table. I was opposite my father. Diana, facing her husband at the other end. Max rose and poured wine from a crystal decanter.

"We are having lamb, so I think this claret will do it credit." This was obviously always Max's part in the proceedings – and was awaiting praise as we took the first sip. My father said:

"Max: this is a lovely claret"

"St Emilion?" (*That was an easy guess,* I thought.)

"Yes!"

Diana interrupted: "Max, stop it. We're not going to spend the whole of dinner with you interrogating poor Edgar on what we are drinking." Max looked shamefaced, but winked at me, as if to repeat what had been obvious as soon as we walked in the house. I said:

"What are you painting at the moment, Max?"

"I'm not."

"You're not?" Had he decided to retire? Surely artists never retire – or that was my romantic view of them. Max continued:

"I'm drawing; returning to basic principles; and copying."

"Copying? Who?"

"Have you heard of Thomas Bewick?"

"Yes. Eighteenth century English artist and woodblock engraver; worked in Newcastle upon Tyne; admired by Ruskin; published History of British Birds." Now it was my turn to be *rodamantade*.

Max was impressed. He said: "Well, Dawn, I thought no one would have remembered old Tom Bewick!"

I didn't pursue it; I didn't want Diana to think I was encouraging her husband to bore the company with his work. I turned my attention to Diana for the rest of the meal, giving the men space to talk whatever kind of shop that interested them. I said to her, "How do you like working for Frances?"

"It's fine; I bring it home and return it by hand – but she's a bit of a dragon, isn't she?"

I grinned. "She can be; she's a mixture of mother hen and Genghis khan, I suppose. I think Frances considers translators and linguists to be head-in-the-clouds scholars who are not really safe to wander the streets of London on their own." I helped Diana clear the table and she shooed the men into the drawing room.

Diana said, "Isn't this terribly old fashioned? The gentlemen leaving the ladies to their coffee while they have a go at the cheese board with a bottle of port. Talking of which, Dawn: shall we have coffee in the kitchen? I've also got a box of Belgian liqueur chocs – then I'll show you around, OK?"

"You are an excellent hostess, Mrs Gilbert."

After this post-prandial indulgence, Diana insisted on giving me what she called the 'grand tour'. I followed her up the stairs; all along the dark-green wallpaper on both landing were works by Max Gilbert – and not necessarily wildfowl; some were small exquisite landscapes he had painted in Scotland and the Lake District. I said to Diana:

"Does your husband paint anything he wants?"

Diana nodded. "He has always considered himself an artisan painter: if a client wants a picture of a factory wall, Max'll paint it. He's very pragmatic, you know. He always remember what

Renoir said, 'An artist is first of all a workman'. But we can't enter the studio; even I am not allowed in there. But let me show you my room."

I followed her on to the next landing. Diana's sanctuary couldn't be more different: pale green walls; white picture rails. Her bed was enormous, with a patterned duvet in pink roses. A large cheval mirror faced her bed. Her wardrobe was pale polished yew. Her tie-back drapes were of patterned silk. Looking out of the window, I could see the quiet street below, but on the opposite wall were hung drawings – all of Diana nude.

She caught my glance. "Whaddya think, Dawn: do they do me justice?"

"Just give me time to take it all in – God, Diana: this room is like a high-class bordello! Especially that one with you bending forward, sticking your tongue out – that's fearfully erotic."

Diana grinned. "So I hoped!" She slid the twin doors aside from the wardrobe and showed off her clothes. "OK?"

There was a long line of dresses, suits, and evening gowns that floated as she flung back the doors.

"My God, Diana: are they all Italian?"

"All from Milan. Rather nice, aren't they?"

"Must have cost a fortune!" And before I could stop myself, I replied, "They so remind me of the gifts from Carlo..."

Diana sat on her bed. "And who, may I ask, is Carlo?" She patted the duvet and I sat next to her. I told her about Carlo, our affaire, of running around Europe after him; and my now realising whether I could continue; how tired I was of it all.

"First of all, Dawn, what you've told me won't go any further – I may be a nosy cow, but I don't blab. OK? And I don't suppose you need unwanted advice from me."

"As a matter of fact, I would."

"Right. First: dump him. This relationship is going nowhere. From what I can tell, he just snaps his fingers, you meet him at some classy hotel, you have lots of sex and champagne, then you're back where you started in London. You're not mistress material, Dawn."

I shrugged. "Well, circumstances may now alter that: I've told Frances that I am no longer prepared to be dragged all over Europe for business conferences. I want to stay in England, and do translation work; I'm fed up with being at everybody's beck and call."

Diana said: "Will your income drop?"

"Yes, but I won't exactly starve. Actually, there is a new opening, if I play my cards right."

"How come?"

"Well, I did a one-off translation at the Revenue and Customs office. I had to trail to the other side of London. It was all a bit spooky. I was locked in a pokey office with this mysterious senior police officer – I think he was a commander in the Special Branch."

"Crikey!"

"But he was very much the old-fashioned gent – Maddox was his name."

Diana suddenly grasped my wrist. "What did you say his name was!"

"Diana, you're hurting!"

She let go. "God, I'm sorry, Dawn."

"What's the problem?"

Diana sighed, then said, "I think there is something you ought to know. But you must swear you won't repeat what I'm going to tell you."

What on earth was this? I retreated, because I thought that she was about to tell me something I didn't *want* to know. I said:

"You don't have to tell me anything that's none of my business." I tried to be flippant: "You and Max haven't been fiddling the tax man, have you?"

Then she told me that when she was a student and worked part-time at a hotel in King's Lynn as a receptionist she was attacked in the staff quarters by a Russian who tried to rape her. Diana defended herself and killed the man. It was self-defence (and I was to find out that she was expert at that). As she flung him over her shoulder he cracked his head on the concrete floor. Then I realised why she became so agitated when I mentioned

Maddox's name, for he was the same Commander for whom I translated the Bill of Lading document, who protected Diana when she worked in the hotel. He must have had some pretty powerful connections. He had brought the Russian ashore from somewhere near Lowestoft and they were staying at the hotel, before travelling on to London. What the Commander was doing, bringing a Russian into the UK secretly, Diana didn't know (or wouldn't tell me), and I didn't ask for more details. What an extraordinary story! It was really rather creepy, getting to know Diana, then discovering that she was guilty of what amounted to manslaughter! And now it seemed that I was going to work for the mysterious Maddox.

Then I spotted a white cotton tunic in her wardrobe; a black sash was tied round its waist. I asked, "Is that an outfit for…"

"Yes: it's my judo gear."

"You're a judoka? A black belt?"

"Yes. I had just been awarded my first black belt when the incident with Boris happened. Just as well," she added calmly, "that the powers-that-be in judo didn't find out. They take bringing the sport into disrepute very seriously. I could have been suspended – or worse."

Really, Diana: that would never do. But what about the poor Russian, who was probably at the bottom of the North Sea? God, the more I learn about my new friend, the warier I was becoming. This was one scary lady; my feelings towards her (I realised now that I did have feelings about Diana) were a mixture of fright and, oddly, as if she were an older sister.

On the journey home, I was the silent one; my father noticed, but wisely said little, except for the usual polite conventions.

"A most enjoyable evening, Dawn! Max was a splendid host – did you know he and his late wife photographed wildfowl in Denmark?"

Even when I lay, tired in my bed, exhausted after the rich dinner and wine, I couldn't get over the evening's surprise news from Diana about her experience in the hotel – was it really true? Did she actually kill the man? What possible reason could she have for making up such a story? She didn't seem like a fantasist: on the contrary, Diana was a girl who had her feet very much on the ground. It was my mentioning the mysterious Maddox that sparked it off. So with visions of Diana in hazardous situations, I fell asleep.

I suppose I was grateful for a quiet weekend with my father (Anne was still in Edinburgh). We did some work on the Codex on the Saturday morning; in the afternoon after lunch my father dozed over a book; I did a few personal chores, then followed my dad's example by falling asleep on my bed.

We went to my father's favourite Italian restaurant for lunch on Sunday, then for a walk in the park in the bright sunshine, enjoying the bustle of children running wild with footballs and kites, most of which barely left the newly-mown grass no matter how hard the kids ran with them. Their parents sat under oak and lime trees, eating sandwiches, drinking wine and lager, keeping half an eye on their offspring. About four o'clock, a black cloud moved ominously over the tree-lined road. My father and I made our way home.

Monday, and the week ahead looked as though it would follow a pattern of our home being peaceful – no callers; very little mail. So Dad and I lost ourselves in the palimpsest (or rather, he did).

I had got into a pleasant, stress-less routine during that fine week (the cloud on Sunday afternoon having drenched the park for 30 minutes moved on, scattering after lightening its flood).

All that changed on Thursday, when Mrs Mills, our cleaner, called me to the telephone.

"Good morning, Miss Hope." It was Commander Maddox. So: my peaceful interlude was coming to an end. I returned his polite greeting, then said:

"And what can I do for you, Commander: another lunch date in a church-yard? We really can't keep meeting like that – people will start to talk."

He ignored me, then said, "Are you free this weekend? It would assist my department if you were." (I could hardly assume that to be an improper suggestion – and therefore give a saucy reply.)

"I believe I am." (*Carlo, where are you?*)

"What I had in mind was for you to have an introduction to the workings of my department. This will necessitate your attending a training weekend, leaving tomorrow afternoon and returning to London on Monday morning. Is that clear, Miss Hope?"

"Yes. But where? And how do I get there? And how do I get my fee?"

A pause, then he said, "Inspector Hibbert will collect you between four and five pm; the destination is confidential…"

"Hold on, mister; I don't go anywhere without telling my father: he's old and not very mobile. What if he should have a fall in the house and not able to reach the phone?"

"What about your aunt? Would she stay?"

All that I'd just told Maddox was an exaggeration, of course: I just wanted to see how far I could push him. I said, "I'll arrange something."

"Very good. By the way, I should pack outdoor clothing: designer dresses would not be appropriate." And he put the phone down.

Outdoor clothing? What did that mean? What was I letting myself in for – some sort of Outward Bound caper? Was I going to work for Customs or the SAS? And how did he know about my aunt? As I walked back to the study, I remembered that he didn't say how much they were paying…

My father said: "Everything all right? You look pensive, Dawn." (My dad would never ask me who it was on the phone.)

"Oh, yes; perfectly all right." Then I told him about Maddox and the mysterious weekend. He listened in silence as I outlined what I might be letting myself in for.

Eventually, he said: "'Let me get this straight, Dawn. First of all you were called into this man Maddox's government office; you translated a mysterious document, for which you were paid a consultant's fee…"

"Which I have yet to receive!"

"…Quite. And now he is saying that he wants you to attend what he calls an induction course into his department."

"Correct."

"Very well. Now: does this mean that you are to be offered full-time employment as – what? A translator? A Customs official?"

"From what I understand, Dad, no. I would be employed as a 'consultant' (your favourite word) for an individual project as when required. It could be quite fascinating, exciting, even. Just think, special agent Hope saving the western world from disaster."

My father frowned. "I do not find the prospect amusing, of my daughter running around the country, getting involved with Customs investigators and detectives – in physical danger."

My frivolous streak sometimes backfired on me – especially with Dad. I hastened to reassure him. "Dad! I shall be perfectly safe. You don't think that a weekend back at college in the country, learning rules and regulations, with early-morning runs will do me any harm, do you?" I was making that up as I went along. I hoped I sounded convincing. And anyway, had he forgotten that I had been wandering around Europe – sometimes on my own – for nearly ten years? The truth was, as you probably gathered from previous observations, that I was getting bored with my life; and the affaire with Carlo, the high living, was beginning to pall. I had asked myself whether I still loved him, and the fact that I had to ask myself that question proved – what?

Next morning, I had forgotten those doubts, and my father didn't mention our conversation. By the time of my rendezvous with John Hibbert had come my father was in the study, poring over his stamp collection. When the doorbell rang, I remembered Maddox's advice about 'designer dresses', so I had decked myself out in jeans (M&S, not Armani) and a sweater. When I opened the door, he was dressed similarly; I made a quick decision. I said:

"Come in and meet my Father; he's always interested when I'm going away with a man for the weekend."

Hibbert pulled a face. "Very funny, Dawn."

I took him into the study, and said to my Father, "Dad, this is Detective Inspector John Hibbert, my escort and protector; isn't that right, John?"

John ignored me and held out his hand. "Hello, sir."

My Father shook it and said (noticing his expression), "Ignore this spoiled child, Inspector. I do. But nice to meet you, all the same." Dad glared at me. "I would advise you to listen and learn and curb your tongue, young woman."

"Yes, Dad." I kissed him, and said, "Give my love to Anne."

"Out! Delinquent."

John and I stood on my doorstep. He asked: "Anne? Or am I being nosy?"

"Yes, you are; but never mind. Anne is Dr Anne Holt, an anthropologist, Dad's lady friend."

"So Professor Hope has a distinguished girlfriend to match his distinction." I didn't reply to that. He said, "Sit in the back." I opened the door and slid on to the seat. Surprised, I saw that someone else was there.

"Hi, Dawn."

It was Diana Gilbert.

Chapter Seven

Diana's Tale

I have returned: yours truly, Diana Hunt[1], as was; now respectable Mrs Diana Gilbert. So what was I doing, sitting in the back of John Hibbert's powerful German car, waiting for Dawn Hope?

So let me start the day after I married Max Gilbert C.B.E., R.A...

In my day dreams I thought, Wow, Mrs Gilbert – Italy! I'll plan it all. First class to Paris: overnight at the George V hotel (and my husband will not forget that!). Simplon Orient Express to Venice, dining in high style, grand piano tinkling in the background while we sipped champagne; and Hercule Poirot bowing over my hand, saying, Madame, you are a lady most formidable!

Well, it wasn't quite like that... But, as usual in Max's household, he left all the arrangements to me, which I carried out with my usual efficiency. It was more like taking the train in the Eurotunnel; not first class, but what they called 'business premier,' not that there was much difference between that and third, to Paris. (And for once the bloody-minded French rail workers were not on strike.) Max hated flying, but loved trains; so here we were, speeding our way to Paris at 190 miles an hour. And I was sitting opposite a distinguished and elegant man who was now my husband. Max was reading The Times, and we were both drinking passable coffee. He must have felt me looking at him, for he lowered the newspaper and said:

"Happy, my dear?"

"Ecstatic, darling."

---

[1] Diana Hunt first appears in an e-book, published in 2011: 'Room Service' by Dian Hunt (me!), available on Amazon, etc.

He grinned. "Then all is for the best in the best of all possible worlds."

"Voltaire?" (Although I wasn't certain that he was quoting correctly.)

"Spot on!" And he returned to his paper. I placed the guide-books I had been studying on the table between us and stared out of the window. *Well*, I pondered, *a little different from the last time I was on my way to Paris, with Melanie, on our naughty weekend;* a couple of college kids playing at being sapphos, and having dinner with two gay American men. My god, that seemed a long time ago. I wondered whether she married that American scientist from Boston? But of course she would – Mummy would have seen to that...

I watched the flat planes of Picardy slide by, and before we were aware of urban life the Gare du Nord came into view.

I smiled at Max and said, "*Bienvenu a Paris, mon cher.*"

"So here we are! How many years is it since I've been to the city of light? Wonderful!" Max folded his newspaper, and stared out of the window, craning his neck. I could see that I had an enthusiastic small boy on my hands: let's hope I could keep up with him.

I had worked out a plan whereby we would stay at a very good hotel near the rail station – but not *too* near a rail station: that is a mistake made by many tourists. I told the taxi-driver to take us to the rue Lafayette – the Ranke hotel: which should open his eyes. For Max and I made an agreement before we left London: that I would organise our journey and choose the hotels in each place we visited over the next three weeks or so. All he knew was that we were going to spend three days in Paris, then take the train to Milan. What he had in mind, of course, was to continue my artistic education. He knew that I'd visited France with a fellow college student – but that was hardly an introduction to French art – something a lot more earthy and sensuous.

The taxi stopped outside the hotel, I paid off the driver, and got a porter to handle our baggage. We stepped inside to a blaze of art deco lighting. "Good god!" said Max, "where have you brought me? Is this a hotel, a bank or a bordello?"

"Probably been all three in its time. C'mon, darling: let's test the bed." (I spoke the latter three words in French.). The concierge tried to hide a smirk.

Max replied, "This is the strangest mixture of decor I have ever seen in a hotel. Why do they have miniature Egyptian mummies in glass cases – are they for sale?"

"They probably expect guests to break the glass and steal them – they will then be hit by the mummies' curse and will have to return year after year until they die." As usual, I was making all this up just to tease Max. (At the same time, I was grateful that I resisted the temptation to book us in at the hotel in the rue Sainte Beuve near the Luxembourg Gardens, where Melanie and I stayed all that long time ago. That would have been too much.)

Max said: "You are a very amusing young lady. Where do we have lunch?"

"I can see that you still have your priorities in order, darling. Follow me." We took the lift to the top floor, the porter deposited our baggage and I tipped him. I knew that Max would be tired after the journey, so I had a cold lunch sent up which was appropriate: it was a warm, early summer's day. Our suite had a balcony; Max drew up a chair and stared out of the double windows, then opened them. He sat with a sketchbook, while I unpacked our bags, removed all my clothes and slipped on a silk peignoir. From our suite we had a distant view of Sacre Coeur; Max had started to sketch it in soft pencil, when I stopped him. He looked up at me. I was sipping rose d'Anjou and had set out lunch on a marble table in front of a leather sofa. He said:

"Mrs Gilbert, when I looked round at you the sunlight shone through your gown; it was most provocative." I poured a glass of wine and passed a plate of smoked salmon to my husband. I said:

"Well, you know me, Max: always the provoker."

We fell asleep, but I had to slide off the bed about an hour later; I was naked and the chill from the open windows had woken me. Max, of course, was still fast asleep – the naughty man, so I joined him under the sheet. So that was more or less how we spent the next two or three days: early rising; coffee and croissants in our room; then tramped the streets of Paris, continuing what Max called my artistic education – the Louvre, the Musee d'Orsay, Rodin.

On the second day we sat under the plane trees in the Luxembourg Gardens (and I didn't feel my past catching up with me) on rickety iron chairs, the sunlight dappling through. It was exactly 10.30: coffee time. I said to Max: "If we were to look down on this scene who would have painted it?"

Max smiled. "No, darling: I want *you* to tell *me*."

"OK, at first I thought Monet; but no, Renoir."

"Full marks! But why?"

"Because if Monet had painted the scene his brush strokes would have been more definite, and perhaps a darker palette. But for Renoir, this would have been a light-hearted scene with lovers sat under the tree."

Max clapped his hands loudly and startled a flock of pigeons who were scavenging around our feet. "My dear Diana, you have a very perceptive eye. I will teach you to draw."

"No you won't. Have you finished your coffee?"

So we spent the remainder of our time in Paris with Max being the lecturer and me being the pupil. We crossed the river to the Musee d'Orsay, and Max insisted on touring every gallery, making comments and throwing questions at me. I loved the d'Orsay – always bathed in light, reflected on its stone plinths; always such a friendly art gallery; which is more than one could say about the Louvre. But by the end of three days I'd had enough of being student/maid-of-all-work/guide and dutiful wife.

The next day we took the first-class express for Milan. I'd also had enough of culture: now it was time for some serious retail therapy. And also, Max was looking tired; he needed to chill out, put his feet up in the hotel for a couple of days. He was happy to do that, saying, "Darling Diana, I shall be perfectly all right. I shall sit in the lounge, observing Italian humanity passing by, reading, sketching and drinking coffee."

"Not too much espresso, Max: it is an unhealthy stimulant."

"Go, child; and don't spend all my money."

So I left Max sprawled on a leather sofa at the Hotel Spadari shortly after breakfast and, purchasing a copy of the fashion magazine, Interni, caught the 10 a.m. bus to Fidenza discount village; when in Milan, do as the shrewd Milanese ladies – don't pay Milan prices for top-quality clothes; take the free coach, and in less than an hour find yourself in the best discount place for top-quality clothes. [So I went for it: Fausto Santini and Ferragamo shoes; and I also came away with an incredibly slinky Missoni knitted suit in caramel that clung like a second skin. Then an evening dress in purple silk from Valentino. Finally, outside is no good unless underneath is attended to (British girls take note). The best is La Perla. Now, I don't have poached-egg tits: I demand support. I bought three 'bodies' in different styles, cream stretched satin, with lace bodice; pink and lace stretched nylon; and just to complete the femme fatale ensemble, a nifty outfit in black and red. These garments fitted, because in Italian shops the serving girls push in your boobs in to make sure; no false modesty there.]

Anyway, after that fashion lesson from yours truly, back to Milan and my beloved, who wasn't where I had left him earlier that morning. But there was a note from Max which the young man in reception handed to me as I walked in. It said:

Diana: I am about to walk off my excellent lunch and visit the Duomo. I hope you had a pleasant morning's shopping.

Ps: Do we have any money left?

Max xxx

Well, yes, Max, we do, and I'm pleased that you had a nice lunch, for it has just dawned on me that I haven't eaten. So I ordered room service; I was tired and hot, and needed a shower. I had prosciutto, fresh rolls, and a pot of Earl Grey tea after my shower, then lay on the bed and dozed.

Max woke me like a prince charming: I was startled: he chuckled, then said:

"I caught you unawares, my sweet. I nearly said 'underwears', but I see you are devoid under the kimono." (It had fallen apart while I was sleeping.)

"Max, you are a naughty old man – and where have you been?" I pulled my robe around me and sat up against the pillows, but the damn thing being silk parted again and showed my chest. Max didn't seem to notice. He threw his jacket on a chair, removed his shoes, and sprawled beside me.

"I have had a most interesting afternoon."

I had a feeling that I was going to get another lecture on Italian art. *Ah, well: I did have a morning's shopping.* I said:

"Really, darling; tell me all about it."

"My first call was the Duomo." He glanced at me. "You got my note.?"

"Yes."

"You know what I mean, of course."

"One could hardly miss it; I passed it on my way to the bus this morning."

"Have you ever seen anything so magnificent?"

"I wasn't particularly impressed, Max."

"No! Of course, you only saw it from the side. Even so..."

"Buildings – especially church buildings – don't impress me: I think of the bloody tyrants who put them up; all in the name of God. As far as I can think – and I don't waste my time considering them – it was the Catholic Church consolidating its power over the poor peasantry."

"Good heavens, Diana. What an outburst! I can see you belonging to the Richard Dawkins school of moral philosophy."

Who? I wasn't being entirely glib: news was coming through at that time about priests sexually assaulting children – and their bishops trying a cover-up. What did they expect when the church enforced celibacy on its clergy? Where did they think all that repressed energy went to? Like many English travellers before me, I was falling in love with this country and its people and its culture. But the dead hand of the Catholic Church's symbolism, crucifixes everywhere, its obsession with sin and death depressed my protestant soul.

I wasn't going to expand on that, instead I said: "Would you like to see what I bought?"

"I suppose I ought to see where all my money went."

"Not all of it, darling."

That evening, we dined at the restaurant Savini in the Galleria Vittoria Emanuele II. The only reason I seem to be showing off in that expensive, elegant establishment, was that I wore my Valentino silk dress. Much to Max's pleasure, I turned a few heads; I remember saying to myself when we married that I would make him proud of me – I did that evening, and until the early hours.

But I won't go into that; after all, I am now a lady (but what happened to the bloody-minded, ambitious, unscrupulous Diana Hunt, as was? Easy: she grew up). The remainder of our time in Milan we spent strolling leisurely in the early summer sun in the centre of the city – Piazza del Duomo; one could hardly avoid it. I even let Max take me in the lift to the cathedral roof; I wasn't to know that I was to witness a tragedy there in the future. But that day I just admired the view which Max was sketching rapidly. And of course I was dragged to the city's greatest treasure – Leonardo's Last Supper in the Cenacolo Vinciano – or what we could see of it; the crowds were horrendous. But we had a heated discussion in a cafe on the piazza afterwards.

"So, Diana, your opinion of one the world's greatest masterpieces." Strangely, I felt he was asking the wrong person.

"I've got mixed feelings, Max."

My husband looked surprised. "Really? Why?"

"It's the restoration argument that has been going on for years that bothers me."

"What! You don't consider that it is worth saving?"

"No: everything has its lifespan: when it's done, it's finished. Like the *The Ambassadors* in the National Gallery. It's very beautiful; but it is not what Holbein painted. In fact, I think it's dishonest." I sipped my coffee while Max absorbed this.

He said: "Diana: that is ridiculous! Just think what you're saying. Thousands of people would never see *The Last Supper or The Ambassadors* if one were to follow your thinking."

"OK, I'll accept *The Ambassadors*, but that sad excuse in the Cenacolo Vinciano – well, by the time somebody's decides something it will be too late. It's Leonardo's fault really."

Max was now amused. He asked:

"And how do you come to that conclusion?"

"Because he painted it in oil. If he had followed a sensible technique-tempera, it might have survived."

"I can see that you have been doing your homework, *cara*."

"If you wondered who has raided your library, it was me. They are all in my boudoir."

"I never go in your boudoir."

"Oh, yes, you do."

Max laughed out loud. "Diana – you are unique."

"Kind of you to say so – as a matter of fact, so are you. Tell you what, why don't we go back to the hotel and I'll take all my clothes off. Would you like that?"

Max looked round quickly, alarmed.

But I didn't make any more complaints in our last few days in Milan. Why should I? I suspect the problem was mine: the old Eve was raising its head. We took the train to Coma, and sat in a waterside cafe and watched tourist boats criss-cross the lake. It was good to get out of the city and to feel the fresher air. The view was hardly spectacular, because there was mist hanging over the water; even so, Max was happy, he had his sketchbook as always on his lap; but just as I was reflecting on the view, a shaft of sunlight broke across the hills and fell gently on the surface of the lake. How suddenly so beautiful. I looked at him while he concentrated on his drawing; and thought, *How on earth, Diana, did you find yourself here? Talk about the wages of sin!* Well, the pay-back had come up trumps for me.

The day before we left Milan was another cultural tour: the Milan museum of modern art; which was fun – well, let me put it like this: Marcel Duchamp's bicycle wheel jammed in a stool is funny. And I think that Max was pleased that I was enjoying myself. We stopped in front of Mussini's *Odalisque*, a painting of a young woman lying on a chaise-longue, naked; the upper part of her body propped against the top curve of the sofa. Max was amused as I stared at it. He asked:

"Well, what do you think?"

I grinned at him. "What do I think? I'm trying to decide whether she's just made love or expecting to."

"She is looking over her shoulder... Do you think it is well painted?"

"Beautifully. Better than Goya's *Naked Maja*. It is obvious – well, obvious to me – that he forgot his anatomy lessons: one tit pointing to the right upwards; the left dropping to the ground." I pointed to the Odalisque. "But this gal is perfect." I suddenly felt my husband's hand on my bottom.

"As perfect as you," he replied.

"Cheeky."

You will have got the message that Max and I were having one helluva time in Italy; and what pleased me especially was that I was perfecting my Italian so quickly. One waiter asked me if I 'came from the South'; that must have been my Norfolk burr coming through. I had planned our route so that our final three destinations – Verona, Padua, and Venice – were taken in that order. (I sometimes wondered if Max ever considered how it was that things ran so smoothly; I mean, did he ever think how he always had clean underclothes and socks? Had he never heard of hotel laundries?)

From where I was now sprawling on my bed at home in London, I could see several photographs taken during our honeymoon. Three of them were in silver frames and rested on my dresser. (I am writing now two months later.) Each was taken in the final cities of our itinerary. There was one of Max with his arm round Juliet's waist, his right hand cupping her breast. He had a big grin on his face. Her right breast shone goldenly, of course, because of the thousands of tourists who had polished the metal effigy down that alley-way in Verona, doing what my husband was doing in the picture. (Blimey, Diana; what have you done to him – led him into a second childhood?)

Oddly, one of the other photographs was taken a couple of hours after the only occasion when we had a short-tempered argument – over, of all things, the Giotto frescoes in the Scrovegni Chapel in Padua. The late morning had become very hot; Max was looking tired as we walked across the park to the chapel; and I didn't particularly want yet another cultural lesson. The chapel was crowded; it was stifling; after ten minutes, I'd had enough. I pushed my way through the mob, taking Max in trail to the exit. He snapped:

"Why did you do that?"

"Because I've had enough of these dreary bloody religious paintings, with all the same theme of death and wailing and those miserable saints and virgins. It gives me the willies. Don't they ever smile?"

"It was ill-mannered of you, Diana."

We hadn't stopped walking, but I could still feel the tension between us. "Yes it was; but at this moment I don't particularly care. The Renaissance is choking me, Max, remember that I have clean laundry to collect, our final packing before Venice – and all I want to do right now is drink a cold beer out of this heat. So if you don't like that idea, Max – tough." We walked together slowly and silently until we reached a cafe. We sat inside the small establishment in front of our beers. After a while, Max turned to me. He said:

"Does that mean we've just had a first row of our married life?"

I had recovered my composure by now. I grinned and said, "Yes, sorry, darling."

"So, we are still friends?"

"Yes, and I still love you."

"I too. So all is well that ends well."

"Of course. But I still think all of Giotto's faces look the same."

"No more iconoclastic remarks, Mrs Gilbert. Tomorrow we shall be in Venice."

And that is where the final photograph was taken: it was of me, sat in the Piazza san Marco outside cafe Florian (away from the pigeons), drinking coffee and absorbed in that day's copy of *Corriere della Sera*. That must have been on the occasion when Max had wandered off to explore the Doge's Palace (all those awful paintings of hell by Bosch!); he had taken the photo on his return when I was absorbed in the newspaper.

I now lay back on my pillows and thought of Italy – the places we had been, what we had seen and disagreed about; Padua wasn't the only occasion; the other art criticism was teasing on my part; it gave Max an opportunity to slap my rear (my husband seemed obsessed by my bum). Max had taken most of the photographs, not only as souvenirs of our trip; but also, I felt, as a source for what could be called an artist's stock reference. If he wanted to paint one of the sights, say, a watercolour (not his usual medium) he had an immediate source. And another thing I had noticed about the scenes was when he had photographed a subject he had 'framed' it in his mind; the whole picture had 'balance', so when it was printed it looked like a 'finished' painting: that was Max, always the professional. *God,* I thought (if he was listening), *I do love him; who would have thought that I could love anyone this much?*

But now I would have to move myself off my very comfortable bed, for I was expecting my step-daughter (Patricia), which was bizarre, because she was only a little older than I. I wondered what her attitude would be, now that the fact that her father had married someone half his age had sunk in? I shrugged. There was nothing I could do about that: I would be the respectful, charming hostess, as usual. At least she was bringing her daughter, Laura – now that would be fun. Thankfully, Max looked well; I opened the French windows on to the terrace, into a Sunday afternoon in midsummer. I had set the scene: light rolled into the dusky living-room, making the prospect inviting. I was wearing a silk flowered dress. Max touched my hand as I moved near the table: he was sat on a corner of the terrace, wearing a panama hat that had seen better days. He didn't let go as I moved when I heard the doorbell. He said:

"Thank you, darling girl."

"Max! Desist– it's the door."

Patricia walked in followed by Laura. We kissed each other chastely. "You look well," she said. Laura hugged my legs.

I said, "Where's Nigel?" (Her husband).

Before she could answer, Laura said, "Daddy's parking the car. Where's grandpa, Diana? Are we having tea? Are we having cake?"

"Shoo, child. Grandpa's on the terrace. Cake, indeed! Certainly not."

"Diana! I always have cake here."

"Too much cake makes your ears fall off."

"No it doesn't! You said that only cold weather makes your ears drop off. You're telling fibs."

I followed Patricia into the living-room. "She hasn't changed, Patricia."

She smiled. "No way; it must be your bad influence."

"Blimey! Am I that bad." Patricia halted and placed her hand on my arm.

"No, of course... is Dad all right? How did he survive the trip?"

"I'll say! I couldn't keep up with him. Dragging me around all those galleries and museums. He ate like a horse, and would only drink the best wine." She and I had a distant, wary relationship, which of course was understandable – a beautiful young woman seducing her father for his money, etc. But I had put her straight about that. Max had proposed to me; not me to him. Whether Patricia believed me when I told her that her father had given this orphan a home and contentment, and wasn't after his money or reflected prestige... well, that was up to her. I could do no more. But that afternoon her attitude had softened. I heard Nigel's footsteps as Patricia greeted her father. He strode to me, a tall, rangy, man with an untidy beard: he reminded me of my first lover, the head waiter at The Ship Hotel, when I was housekeeper; the time when the Russian illegal émigré died at my hands. I pushed the thought from my mind.

"Hello, Diana! You have returned from the fleshpots of Italy, leading my pa-in-law astray, no doubt." He brushed my cheek with his beard. I said:

"More like the other way around, Nigel; the old devil."

We clustered round the iron, glass-topped table. I poured tea; they helped themselves to sandwiches. Laura sat on her father's knee, and drank orange juice. I turned to Nigel. "So," I asked, "where do you go from here – Africa, India...?"

He shook his head. "Nowhere. No more pioneering. I shall be working out of the School, researching and lecturing." (He meant the London School of Hygiene and Tropical Medicine.).

Max said: "No doubt Pat and Laura will be relieved, Nigel – having you home."

I wondered whether there was an edge to Max's remark; if there were, it wasn't noticed. Patricia glanced at her father then her husband. "Nigel's really had enough, haven't you, darling?"

"Yes: it's not the work. It's mainly the frustration, with interference both from host governments and medical charities. They all want a slice of the action – I wasn't cut out for politics! And also that fool of a Pope interfering in our AIDS prevention program. It's bad enough trying to persuade African tribal savagery, without the Church and its medieval attitude. But that's only one of the problems – even if it gets the most publicity. Malaria, yellow fever, HIV/hepatitis B is still... Sorry, I seem to be going on and on."

But I said: "I get the impression, Nigel, that slipshod hygiene was the reason for those outbreaks in our hospitals."

"That's right. They got careless! The School does not have 'Hygiene' in its name for nothing."

Patricia interjected. "Anyway, enough doom and gloom: we have some good news for you." I knew what she was going to say. She looked at her father. "You're going to be a grandpa again."

"What! That's wonderful news." For a split second I felt a stab of jealousy, and I also caught the brief look of triumph, which I am sure was directed at me. The silence was broken by Laura – having finished her tea – said: "Mummy said that our baby might be here for Christmas." I noticed the 'our'.

I said: "Does that mean that you ordered it from Tesco, like a turkey?"

I got a withering look from Laura. "No, silly – it grows in Mummy's tummy."

I thought I'd better get into her good books. "Laura, would you like to see my new Italian dress?"

She jumped off her father's knee. "Yes, please! Can we go now?"

Laura ran in front of me and clattered up the stairs. "Slowly, please, Laura!" That was her mother, not me; but I followed with:

"You heard what Mummy said." Laura loved my room: it was an Aladdin's cave to her, mainly, I suppose, because I had scarves, shawls, and silk peignoirs draped everywhere. (I was clean, but very untidy.) Laura found one of my floppy hats and plonked it on her head. She stared at herself in the long oval mirror. I draped a long chiffon scarf over her shoulders. She twirled to the left and then to the right, then looked up at me and said:

"I look like one of those ladies at horse races I've seen on the television, don't I, Diana?"

Who? I was slow, then I realised she meant Ascot. "You do, Laura." She continued to make free with my things, and I got pleasure by just watching her – pleasure mixed with what amounted to a strange sadness, remembering her mother's announcement about her pregnancy. God; I hope I wasn't getting broody. And I also recall Max – all those months ago in King's Lynn – saying that he wasn't affected by sexual desire: that he was old: that he could do drawings of me nude without being aroused. At the time, I thought, how very odd (I was in his room at the Ship Hotel). I had defiantly removed my blouse and bra, and stood in front of him while he was drinking a glass of claret, with his sketchbook on his knee. I thought I was being brazen and cocking-a-snook at this upper-class gentleman. Later, I realised that all I had done was make myself look silly. (Incidentally, when we became engaged I very soon changed his mind about not being aroused – much to his surprise.) But motherhood? That would just not be on: Max becoming a father again in his mid-sixties? Ridiculous. Oh, *sod* it.

Laura eventually got tired of her game and wanted to go back to her parents; but I had one more surprise for her. I reached under the bed and drew out an oblong box. It was wooden, highly polished with a top of burr veneer. Inscribed on the lid in curly letters was the word Venezia. I placed it on the duvet and Laura scrambled across.

"What's that, Diana?"

"That is for you, mischief – a souvenir from Italy, from me." Her eyes popped, her mouth dropped open, and for once she was speechless. I had put some old bits of costume jewellery in the box – it measured about 12 inches by 8 inches – just the sort of sparkly stuff she would love. I heard Laura run down the stairs, shouting,

"Mummy, Daddy, see what Diana's given me!" I lay back on my bed and closed my eyes, because I had the feeling that if I didn't I would start to cry. *You silly cow, Diana,* I thought. And then Dawn Hope came into mind, and her Italian lover: what on earth was an educated, clever, attractive blonde doing getting involved with an Italian crook (Italian *and* a millionaire, ergo, crook). The same reason that we all do it – we had the need at the time: sex reared its ugly head, and Nature took over. I bet he bought her diamonds (not costume jewellery!), silk undies, and clothes from Dolce & Gabbana.

I slid off the bed and returned to my wifely duties.

Monday, Monday. Quiet normality. I was due at the Agency, returning a batch of translations; Max vanished into his studio. Before I left, I told Max where the flask of coffee and sandwiches were by shouting through the studio door; but he didn't answer – he never did. I followed the crush on the Tube that Monday, and as I walked out of the station to the Strand I thought about Dawn – and her meeting with Commander Maddox. Now that was scary. It had really shaken me. Talk about the past catching up with me! A coincidence? I hoped so; but I couldn't get the picture out of my mind when that thug had attacked me in the cellar of the Ship Hotel in Lynn. Also, after I had defended myself and he died – I was scared of my own skill; in that I was using judo techniques in a dangerous situation. That was no controlled contest situation in a judo club under the beady eyes of a referee and mat judges. That was real; it ended in a messy death. I was still thinking about Maddox when I reached the Agency and knocked on Frances's door; she beckoned to me and waved me to a chair.

"Well, well, the wanderer returns: how was Italy, Mrs Gilbert? Thank you for the postcard, by the way. A nice picture of Venice. Thank you for writing in Italian! Not much about your trip, but quite a lot about what you had to eat and drink."

I passed her the batch of work. The trouble with this woman was that she reminded me of Maddox. Frances continued, "Are you still willing to offer your services to this agency now you have married such a distinguished gentleman?"

"If you continue this level of sarcasm, Frances, I'll tell you where you can stick your work – you know, where the sun doesn't shine."

There was stunned silence, then Frances laughed out loud. "Touché!" (That was the rough Norfolk girl coming out in me.) I said:

"Well, if there is nothing further…"

Frances wore her spectacles on a gold chain round her neck. She plonked them on her nose and ruffled paper. "There is one thing you can do for me today."

"Of course. I can cancel my luncheon engagement with the Queen."

Frances didn't fall for that one. "I understand that you have become quite friendly with Dawn Hope?"

Where was this leading? I said, "Yes: Max and my father have also become quite friendly. Clever girl, Dawn, isn't she?"

"Indeed: she comes from a talented family…" Then she changed tack. "Look, could I use you as a messenger-girl? I've got some documents that have to be returned to the Royal Courts. Would you mind dropping them off?" She smiled. "It would also be a nice walk for you this sunny morning."

"How kind, Frances." It was a heavily sealed package, addressed to some clerk or other; I placed it carefully in my shoulder bag and fastened it firmly. On the way, I thought about my 'friendship' with Dawn. Was that the way to describe our relationship? I suppose it was; but we didn't know each other very well. Even so, she had opened up about that Italian boyfriend: I was convinced that he was just using her. How could a smart woman like that fall for such a man? That was a pointless question: since when did brains come into the equation? *You should know, Diana.*

I strolled down the Strand to the Old Bailey (with a kind of independent air). I always thought the old building looked more like a Victorian church, with all that ugly revived Gothic. But

I'd never entered it, so I climbed the steps and thought, *Here goes.*

There was an officious little man with an ID tag round his neck wearing a dark uniform half a size too large for him who was checking bags. I waited impatiently while he fingered the package that Frances gave me. Then he nodded and waved me on. I said, "Next time, a 'thank you' would be nice." I approached a uniformed police sergeant.

"Can I help you, madam?" I showed him the package and he said.

"Ah, yes. Would you follow me, please?"

I replied: "How nice to see some manners."

He smiled, and I followed to the rear of the building-through different offices (all closed) and a robing room. He knocked on a door at the end of a corridor, then opened it. I walked in.

"Good morning, Diana."

It was Commander Maddox. I didn't believe that I was seeing what was sitting in front of me: the same man I had told Dawn of only recently; the same pepper-and-salt suit; the same check shirt and club tie; the same highly-polished brogues – from all those ages ago. It was my past catching up with me: the one who knew that I had killed the Russian; who had covered my tracks. And now he had returned to haunt me.

"Bloody hell!"

"Please don't be alarmed, Diana. Sit down; make yourself comfortable." There was another person in that small, shabby, but cosy room; a tall young man in a pale grey suit, who said nothing.

"Make myself *comfortable*! Don't be *alarmed*! What the *fuck* do you think you're playing at Maddox? I'm sent on a wild goose-chase by my boss – I suppose she's one of your hooligans – then I'm confronted by the last person I want to see. Why? Why? Tell me now, or I'm straight out of here." I noticed that the young man was standing by the door. "Also, if that oaf tries to stop me, I'll either break his arm, or he'll end up in a heap in that corner."

Maddox looked at the man. "You see, Inspector Hibbert: all I told you about Diana Hunt – sorry, Mrs Gilbert – was true."

I glared at him again. "You didn't answer my question!"

Strangely, after my blast of bad language and annoyance, I didn't really feel angry. What went swiftly though my mind was, *Did Dawn Hope have anything to do with spying on me?* Because obviously someone had. But, before I married Max I had become a semi-public figure for a while after the auction of some of his drawings and watercolours in aid of cancer research.

But this was pointless speculation. I sat silently after my outburst, and after it Maddox came straight to the point; he wanted to employ me, attached to his department as an interpreter and investigator for H.M. Revenue and Customs. This idea of hopping between Special Branch and Customs seemed like a grey area to me. What were they trying to do – save money by employing part-time freelancers?

Maddox said: "Because of your unique qualifications, I am asking whether you would be willing to undertake occasional projects for my department. I think you would find them interesting – even adventurous. And you would have the satisfaction of knowing you would be serving your country in – ah – dangerous times."

"That was quite a speech, Commander. Let me get this straight. You want me, a respectable married woman, married to a distinguished, wealthy artist. Let's get something very clear: I am no longer the Diana Hunt of the Ship Hotel: the college girl. Now: would you like an interpreter? An investigator? An assassin?"

Maddox leant forward and stared (for a moment I though he was looking at my legs; I automatically pulled at the hem of my skirt). He said quite seriously:

"I don't think we would want you to kill anyone, Diana." He looked across at Hibbert. "Do you, Inspector."

His assistant shook his head. Then said: "Mrs Gilbert is an excellent linguist, sir; and we know of course that she has just earned her second degree black belt at the Budokwai."

God, is there anything these two didn't know about me? This was scary. I said:

"I don't take kindly to all this prying into who or what I now am. Do you want to know what colour my undies are today, Commander?" Hibbert smiled; Maddox looked pained, but asked:

"Do you think you might consider the proposal, Diana?"

"And what do you propose I say to my husband? 'Oh, by the way, dear. I shall be away for a couple of days because my country needs me to catch terrorists and drug smugglers. There is also a possibility that I may have to assassinate one of them. But don't worry, I'll be back in time for tea...'"

I thought over Maddox's reply as I retraced my steps down the Strand with my head still buzzing, bumping into the lunchtime crowds, in the midday heat. I was wearing sunglasses, but they didn't stop me from feeling wobbly. I needed nourishment. So I found St Martins Court and joined the chattering classes in J. Sheekey's restaurant, only the place was half empty and there was no chattering. This place amused me, with its bright red painted and gold sign above the window; it reminded me of the old-fashioned Woolworths store when I was a child in King's Lynn. I ordered a platter of fruits-de-mer and a large glass of Provencal rose.

"May I join you?" God help us. It was John Hibbert.

"Are you stalking me, Inspector?" He sat opposite me. I said: "Don't tell me you fancy me?"

Hibbert smiled. "My interest is purely professional. If you don't mind, Diana, I'd like a chat out of sight of my boss."

"And I'm supposed to believe that, John? That you won't report our conversation; where I might be indiscreet about my past? What about my lovers; shall we start there?"

"For goodness' sake, Diana; stop talking about sex. And please listen for once. If you're going to work for the Department you'll have to learn to keep your trap shut."

"I never said I would. I said I would think about it. And if you continue to be rude and macho, you can leave now."

He started to rise then sat down. He shrugged. "Sorry."

"So I should think. I'll forgive you if you buy lunch."

Hibbert grinned. "You have got a nerve, haven't you, Mrs Gilbert?"

"You'd better believe it. Put the lunch down to expenses."

Of course I had not agreed to work for Maddox: but I suppose the thought of adventure – secret or otherwise – appealed to me. The old Diana was still there, somewhere, I suppose. *'The colonel's lady and Rosie O'Grady are sisters under the skin'.* Well, not quite, Mr Kipling. But you know what I mean.

I didn't reach home until early afternoon; Max was sitting on the patio, looking across our small garden, the sunlight touching his profile, when I arrived. He didn't see me at once. I crept up on him, putting my hands on his shoulders. He touched my hands, then lowered them.

I said, "How was your day, darling?"

"Lazy. I did little drawing. Just reading. Your timing is perfect... but how was yours? Have you brought work home?"

"No. A handsome young man bought me lunch."

"Did he now?"

I pulled up a chair beside him. 'And I have received a proposition."

Max stared. "I can see that I should not let you loose on your own."

I grinned at him, then kissed him. "Shall we have a glass of wine?"

"That would be nice, then you can tell me more about your adventure." We drank cool sauvignon Blanc.

Max then demanded: "Come along, errant wife: confess." I felt his hand slide up my skirt.

I said: "Behave, or I won't tell you anything." He left his hand where it landed, half way along my thigh; but now it was still.

He replied: "You know that I have a strong professional interest in your smooth, beautiful skin."

"Really, Max. I don't think I should have married you: I'm obviously a bad influence."

He moved his hand away.

"That's better. Now pay attention. When I arrived at the Agency, Frances sent me on an errand."

Then I gave Max an edited version of my encounter with Duncan Maddox. For obvious reasons, I didn't mention that portion of my past when I first met Maddox at the Ship Hotel in King's Lynn. Looking back, it seems bizarre that my life was changed both by my Russian attacker in the basement of the hotel (who died nastily for his trouble); even more so, of course, meeting Max by the simple task of taking clean linen to his room.

My husband listened to my shortened account of the morning's meeting, then said: "Let me get this straight, Diana. You went to the Old Bailey to deliver a confidential package to some mysterious person who turns out to be a senior officer at Scotland Yard, who then offers you part-time employment as a translator to accompany police and customs officials when they apprehend suspected criminals – drug smugglers, terrorists, or whatever?"

"Yes."

"Good heavens. And what was your answer?"

"I haven't given one. I needed to speak to you first."

Max was silent for a while, then said, "What do you want to do?"

I hesitated, but that was enough for my husband to say, "The idea of chasing round the country after crooks appeals to you, doesn't it?"

I nodded. "But I won't if you object, Max. I'll forget it. Immediately. Out of hand."

He said: "I appreciate that it must be rather dull for you here at times. I'm stuck in my studio most days, hardly ever appearing…"

"Living with Max Gilbert? You must be joking!"

Max laughed. "Seriously, though – do you want to take this on? I should be concerned about your safety, of course…"

"I'm more concerned about you, Max. If I'm away for days at a time…"

"How will I manage? I'm hardly decrepit!" This sort of exchange between husband and wife (sniping, teasing, affectionate banter) went on for some time, until Max said he was hungry, so I heated the supper I had prepared that morning.

But the prospect of adventure never really left my mind all evening. Later that night I slid out of bed – leaving Max sleeping – and tip-toed naked to my room to find a robe. I slid my toes into a pair of *zori* and tread silently down the stairs. Entering the sitting-room in the dark, I pulled back the drapes from the French windows and allowed the light from the full moon to flood the sitting-room; the night was very still. The scene looked like a Hokusai woodcut print.

I looked up at the still, brilliant full moon, and thought, *So, Diana, was this payback time for Commander Maddox? Quo Vadis?*

Chapter Eight

London

The following morning, after letting the idea germinate overnight (although of course I had decided what to do before I fell asleep), I dressed in one of my best outfits, the girl-on-her-way-to-the-top ensemble: red Armani suit with very short skirt, cross lapel jacket with a low neckline; nearly decent white silk shirt; my feet shod in red killer heels. I looked at myself in the long mirror and thought, *Do I look tarty?* And decided that I nearly did. As I passed by his study, my dad blinked at me.

He said: "I hope that the Agency staff are not too overwhelmed by your personality, Dawn."

"The Agency does not have the pleasure of my company this morning, father: I'm off on a secret assignment with MI5. The future of civilization is at stake."

"And you presumably are hoping to have the psychological advantage over the foe?"

"No: I'm the distraction so James Bond can shoot the villain – but I should be back by this evening for high tea."

He looked me up and down again. "All I can say is that I hope you do not bring any of your ruffian friends with you: I am expecting two members of the philatelic society later this afternoon."

I rechecked my shoulder bag before closing the door behind me – folding umbrella; plastic mac; cell-phone; notebook. (I wasn't going to be caught out like last time when John Hibbert rescued me, much to my embarrassment.) I looked up at the sky. The sun shone, but there one or two black clouds lurking in the distance. The freak heat wave that had persisted over the previous fortnight was still with us, but thunder and cloudbursts were forecast. I left the house and headed to the Tube. I got out at Bond Street and walked the rest of the way to Park Mansions. They had erected five-foot tall railings all round the building, painted black with gold spikes. A small courtyard led to the two enormous doors. I pressed the bell. The concierge answered. "Good morning. How may I help you?"

Well, that was a considerable improvement on my previous visit. "Good morning. This is Dawn Hope, Mr Palladio's colleague." The buzzer sounded and the doors swung open. I walked across the marble floor and the concierge moved from behind his stand. "Is Mr Palladio in…?"

"I'm afraid not, Miss Hope. I believe he is still in Rome."

"Well what about Mr Osbaldiston?"

The black man smiled. "Neither is he, Miss."

"Damn, I have some papers… look, I have my own key. Is it OK if I go up?"

"Of course, you know how the lift operates?"

"Sure. And thank you."

"You're welcome."

So, neither of them was in the building. Good. I took the lift to the top (6th floor) and walked into a deep-pile carpet and glanced up and down the corridor. It was very quiet. Did anybody at all live here? Had anyone seen me? And why was I playing these silly games with myself? Of course people lived here; it was the middle of the morning and they would be out. (*Shut up, Dawn.*)

Carlo's apartment door slid open easily, but by its weight, slowly. Once again I stood inside the room and listened and looked, taking in the contents and the atmosphere. The first thing I noticed was that the air smelled stale; the room was stuffy. I walked across to the nearest long window, drew back a net curtain and tried to open it. It took a lot of effort, and even then would only open a couple of inches. Was the air conditioning working?

The main living room was still decked out in the modern Italian minimalist style (why do they all try to adopt the new boutique hotel furnishings?). The only addition was a large, deeply polished yew-wood desk, behind the cream sofa, and set against the far window. It had a red leather inlaid top, and carried a flat-screen computer and telephone. I lifted up one of the pens in the desk set: Mont Blanc, of course. There were two bedrooms off the corridor. I inspected the larger: silk drapes, fitted sliding wardrobes. Expecting to find clothes hung, I was disappointed: the cupboards were bare as were the drawers. (I was expecting to find one of Carlo's suits at least; and perhaps also a couple of silk nighties from some tramp he might have brought with him from Milan.) The rest of my search revealed the same. In the kitchen-diner: shiny utensils, unused; clean glass dining table. The bathroom, the same: acres of sliding glass doors, behind which were two shower heads; even the basins were glass. There was one final search – the computer.

All the drawers at the knee-hole desk were not locked; but they contained nothing but the usual office junk (stapler, ballpoint pens, notebooks, unused). I sat back on the black swivel chair, and pondered. *Carlo, where are you, and why has this place never been used?* I switched on the computer, but I couldn't get anything except to Google British and European newspapers, and the usual junk. I tried his company's site; but it came up with, 'ACCESS DENIED'. I tried typing his full name: same reaction.

Then I had an idea. I played with a combination of three words:

Segreto

Alba

Speranza.

At the second try I hit the jackpot, and gained access. Clever old me and sentimental old Carlo. The combination was *segreto alba* – secret dawn. I trawled through his private papers (not very nice of me, was it?). A lot of it was copies of correspondence through his companies – letters to fellow directors; decisions for further investment. I noticed that the negotiations for the Spanish investment had ground to a halt; perhaps Carlo had listened to me after all.

And then I hit upon something very intriguing – and just the sort of thing that would interest me. It was a list of famous paintings, mainly from the fifteenth, seventeenth, and nineteenth centuries. And I knew that they all had one thing in common – they had been stolen and never recovered.

So why would Carlo be interested in such criminal activities? For instance, the latest date-wise of a stolen painting was *The Concert*, by Vermeer, which showed two young women and an older man. One woman was seated at a type of keyboard (a virginal?); the other, singing from a sheet of paper. One cannot tell what the man was doing because his back was to the viewer. This was stolen in 1990 from the Isabella Stewart Gardner Museum, in Boston, USA. It had never been recovered.

Just think for a moment. Vermeer's output was a mere 30-odd paintings, and the public was highly unlikely to ever see *The Concert* again. Not only that, but Carlo had listed works by Raphael (stolen by the Nazis in Cracow for Goering's collection); Van Eyck; Michelangelo; Ramsay; Rubens – just reading the list made me cross. *Carlo: what are you up to?*

Underneath this list were comments and questions where they might be – and they were addressed to his son, Aldo. I had now had enough of this.

I needed to think. I printed off the pages, found a large envelope and stuffed them in my shoulder bag. I switched down the computer, tidied the desk and left the apartment.

There was a cafe I frequented just off Bond Street. I ordered a latte and sipped it thoughtfully. Why had I gone through that rigmarole? *Don't kid yourself, Dawn: you were beginning to miss Carlo again, damn him.* But what would I find if we met up again after all these months? Not a lot, I suspected. Business would come first with Carlo, and now he was mixing with that crew surrounding Berlusconi. An MEP, indeed! I opened my cell-phone, and waited.

"Good morning, Mrs Gilbert."

Diana laughed down the line. "Oh, hi, Dawn. How are you?"

"Fine. Look, Diana, can we meet up; I've got something I'd like to discuss with you."

"Sounds mysterious. Anything to do with the Department?"

"No."

"OK: how about lunch tomorrow. Fifth floor, Harvey Nicks, 12 noon."

"Great. Thanks, Diana." (I only hoped she was paying.)

"Don't be daft. Love to see you."

So far, so…? This cloak-and-dagger stuff was all very well, but I was still a working woman with bills to pay. So next stop was the Agency. I needed to speak to Frances. As I climbed the steps, I wondered what she would say. Frances beckoned me into her office; I sat in front of her desk, crossed my legs, and said, "I've got a bone to pick with you, Mrs Brooke – or should I call you 'M', or Miss Moneypenny?"

Frances laughed. "You've been watching too many old Bond movies on the telly."

"You've got a nerve, Frances. So you're Maddox's sister, are you?"

"I am. Sorry about the deception. Duncan sometimes has to go about things in a rather underhand way. After that work you did translating the bill of lading he was very impressed. So he sounded me out…"

"Well bully for him. God help us, he's a snooty devil. I thought people like him went out with Rudyard Kipling."

Frances looked me up and down. "I hope you are wearing something under that skirt."

"Briefly. Now: do you have any work for me?"

"Get us a couple of coffees from the deli round the corner, and I'll see what I can find."

"But I've already had coffee."

"Scoot."

Why did I put up with all this from Frances – and now her brother! However, she dumped a pile of Italian clothes catalogues on me just to shut me up. I ploughed slowly through these. Who would have thought that I could be bored with descriptions of Italian clothes – well, me for a start. It was a job of listings, stock numbers, and no illustrations. It was like reading a telephone directory. I had a late lunch, then told Frances, grumpily, that I was taking the remainder home.

"Well, don't leave them on the Tube."

As I approached the house, I could see my father through his study window (which was on the right-hand side of the front door). He was sitting at his desk looking through a large, free-standing magnifier at was presumably a page of postage stamps.

Stood next to him was an elderly man, peering over my father's shoulder. They were both perfectly still. Then I had a strange feeling, as if, for a moment, time stopped; I felt as if I was looking at a painting – perhaps Vermeer's *The Astronomer*; a still life with human figures.

Then the delicious moment went. My father looked up, saw me, and waved. I climbed the steps to the front door. In the privacy of my bedroom, I spread the sheets from Carlo's office (ignoring Frances's work), reading again the letters between Carlo and his son Aldo, who was the sales manager for one of his father's companies. But the correspondence dealt with normal business transactions – it was more personal; it was Carlo asking his son where he was on certain days; times when Aldo should have been in his office or at a meeting or seeing clients. Aldo's replies were vague, trying to persuade his father at the same time that he was dealing with other aspects of business. He didn't convince me; and it was obvious that he wasn't impressing his father.

I had printed off the stock repros of the Vermeer paintings separately; but what was frustrating was that there was no obvious connection with the correspondence and the paintings. The details of the paintings were in the public domain: nothing unusual there. I decided to leave it until I had spoken to Diana at lunchtime tomorrow. I had had enough for one day. There was basketball practice that evening. That would clear my head. As I ran down the stairs in my tracksuit, my father emerged from his study, alone.

"All alone?" I asked.

"Dawn! Yes and a very pleasant day. How was yours?"

"Half intriguing, the other half tedious."

"Normal, in fact." He looked me up and down. "Basketball, I assume?"

"Yes; maybe the exercise will restore my sanity."

"I'm sure… one moment, Dawn!" My father strode, stick in hand, to the bureau in the hall. "A mysterious parcel, for which I had to sign, arrived shortly after you left. Delivered by a chap wearing some sort of dark-blue uniform and riding a motor-bike."

He was obviously impressed by this; and also immediately assumed it was something to do with the Government department to which I had committed myself. He said, "I'll leave you to it, Dawn," and then made his way to the sitting room. The package was about the size of an A4 envelope and an inch thick; brown paper; stiff parcel tape all over. It was difficult to unwrap, and needed a sharp pair of scissors. I pulled out a five-page document. It was headed HM REVENUE AND CUSTOMS. There then followed a detailed description of my conditions of employment on an ad hoc basis. I scanned the pages quickly; from what I could tell it was in the usual Civil Service jargon.

But also from the package I pulled a small black plastic wallet, folded in two. When I opened it I looked at a photo of myself behind clear plastic. It also identified who I was and my authority. On the opposite side there was stamped in gold a crown over a portcullis. So, now I was official! An employee of a government department, with an ID that would gain me access where even angels feared to tread. The doorbell rang. It was Jonathan's wacky girlfriend, Rebecca, accompanied by him and another boy. She was dressed – like me – in a green track suit with the college sports centre badge. I stared at the boys, and said:

"Oh, hi, Rebecca. But what are these two doing here? This is a girl's night out."

Jonathan and the other boy were stood on the pavement looking shifty; Rebecca looked down. "Oh, the other one's Danny, he's Jonno's mate." Danny smiled weakly.

"Hullo."

"You didn't answer my question."

Jonathan said. "We thought we might be able to pick up some tips – we know how good the ladies' basketball team is, don't we, Danny?" Danny nodded his head, but said nothing. Jonathan spoke for him: "Course not: Danny's a runner – cross-country; let's him think."

"Think about what?" I asked.

At last Danny spoke for himself. "Equations."

"Equations!"

"Yes, Miss Dawn: differential equations."

Jonathan broke in. "He's always thinking about bloody maths; he's a nutter."

The Asian boy glared at his friend and said, "Well you know nothing."

Rebecca got fed up with all this. "They are accompanying us under sufferance, and carrying our kit. They've also got to be quiet while we practice – isn't that right, Danny?"

Jonathan's inchoate pal nodded his head vigorously.

I said, "And I don't know why they put up with you, Rebecca." Danny just stared at me with large brown sad eyes.

Rebecca looked at the hapless boys. "I think they only come along so they stare at our legs and hope we'll show our knickers."

Jonathan blushed. "No we don't! And you can carry your own rotten kit bag." He threw it to the ground.

"Gosh, you do make a fuss, Jonno."

He scowled. "Well you can please yourself. Come on, Danny. Some of the lads are kicking a ball about over there." And they ran off, Danny in the lead.

I recalled what Jonathan's mother, Susan, said about this leggy, frizzy-haired girl – "My poor boy doesn't stand a chance; he calls her a bossy cow, but not to her face. She's not the sort of girl one says 'no' to."

"It's a wonder you allow her in the house."

"Oh, she's perfectly well mannered, considerate and charming. And never embarrasses Johnathan in my presence."

"Well, if you don't mind my saying so, Susan – what does she see in your son?"

Susan laughed. "God knows."

I am recalling this entire episode because in some odd way it seemed to follow in my mind about Carlo; not the things I had stolen from his office; but the remembrance of him. Of our times together: God – he was wonderful. Why did I walk away when he tried to set me up in the luxury Mayfair apartment? Well of course I knew the answer to that; and my reasons at the time were correct. But then of course Carlo did not stand still; I suppose what really made me mad at him was the fact that he ignored my reasons. And he was supposed to love me! Or was it because I was so physically different to those lustrous Italian women; the pure blonde with the pink creamy skin? But I can feel as guilty as anyone; meaning that I came from a privileged background with the brains and looks that could make me behave like a spoiled brat if I didn't get my own way.

By the time I got back from the sports centre that evening I felt that I had things in proportion, and after a shower and supper I thought about Carlo again: I made a quick decision and sent him an email. Let's see what sort of response I got. As regards the information I had 'retrieved' from him – well, I would leave that until I had spoken to Diana. And of course the exercise had done me good: basketball, apart from its fast bursts of speed, takes hard concentration, so that night I fell into a deep and dreamless sleep with no thoughts of Carlo, Maddox or anyone else.

Monday, and the week ahead looked as though it would follow a pattern of our home being peaceful – no callers; very little mail. So Dad and I lost ourselves in the palimpsest (or rather, he did).

I had got into a pleasant, stress-less routine during that fine week (the cloud on Sunday afternoon having drenched the park for 30 minutes moved on, scattering after lightening its flood).

All that changed on Thursday, when Mrs Mills, our cleaner, called me to the telephone.

"Good morning, Miss Hope." It was Commander Maddox. So: my peaceful interlude was coming to an end. I returned his polite greeting, then said:

"And what can I do for you, Commander: another lunch date in a church-yard? We really can't keep meeting like that – people will start to talk."

He ignored me, then said, "Are you free this weekend? It would assist my department if you were." (I could hardly assume that to be an improper suggestion – and therefore give a saucy reply.)

"I believe I am." (*Carlo, where are you?*)

"What I had in mind was for you to have an introduction to the workings of my department. This will necessitate your attending a training weekend, leaving tomorrow afternoon and returning to London on Monday morning. Is that clear, Miss Hope?"

"Yes. But where? And how do I get there? And how do I get my fee?"

A pause, then he said, "Inspector Hibbert will collect you between four and five pm; the destination is confidential…"

"Hold on, mister; I don't go anywhere without telling my father: he's old and not very mobile. What if he should have a fall in the house and not able to reach the phone?"

"What about your aunt? Would she stay?"

All that I'd just told Maddox was an exaggeration, of course: I just wanted to see how far I could push him. I said, "I'll arrange something."

"Very good. By the way, I should pack outdoor clothing: designer dresses would not be appropriate." And he put the phone down.

Outdoor clothing? What did that mean? What was I letting myself in for – some sort of Outward Bound caper? Was I going to work for Customs or the SAS? And how did he know about my aunt? As I walked back to the study, I remembered that he didn't say how much they were paying…

My father said: "Everything all right? You look pensive, Dawn." (My dad would never ask me who it was on the phone.)

"Oh, yes; perfectly all right." Then I told him about Maddox and the mysterious weekend. He listened in silence as I outlined what I might be letting myself in for.

Eventually, he said: "'Let me get this straight, Dawn. First of all you were called into this man Maddox's government office; you translated a mysterious document, for which you were paid a consultant's fee…"

"Which I have yet to receive!"

"…Quite. And now he is saying that he wants you to attend what he calls an induction course into his department."

"Correct."

"Very well. Now: does this mean that you are to be offered full-time employment as – what? A translator? A Customs official?"

"From what I understand, Dad, no. I would be employed as a 'consultant' (your favourite word) for an individual project as when required. It could be quite fascinating, exciting, even. Just think, special agent Hope saving the western world from disaster."

My father frowned. "I do not find the prospect amusing, of my daughter running around the country, getting involved with Customs investigators and detectives – in physical danger."

My frivolous streak sometimes backfired on me – especially with Dad. I hastened to reassure him. "Dad! I shall be perfectly safe. You don't think that a weekend back at college in the country, learning rules and regulations, with early-morning runs will do me any harm, do you?" I was making that up as I went along. I hoped I sounded convincing. And anyway, had he forgotten that I had been wandering around Europe – sometimes on my own – for nearly ten years? The truth was, as you probably gathered from previous observations, that I was getting bored with my life; and the affaire with Carlo, the high living, was beginning to pall. I had asked myself whether I still loved him, and the fact that I had to ask myself that question proved – what?

Next morning, I had forgotten those doubts, and my father didn't mention our conversation. By the time of my rendezvous with John Hibbert had come my father was in the study, poring over his stamp collection. When the doorbell rang, I remembered Maddox's advice about 'designer dresses', so I had decked myself out in jeans (M&S, not Armani) and a sweater. When I opened the door, he was dressed similarly; I made a quick decision. I said:

"Come in and meet my Father; he's always interested when I'm going away with a man for the weekend."

Hibbert pulled a face. "Very funny, Dawn."

I took him into the study, and said to my Father, "Dad, this is Detective Inspector John Hibbert, my escort and protector; isn't that right, John?"

John ignored me and held out his hand. "Hello, sir."

My Father shook it and said (noticing his expression), "Ignore this spoiled child, Inspector. I do. But nice to meet you, all the same." Dad glared at me. "I would advise you to listen and learn and curb your tongue, young woman."

"Yes, Dad." I kissed him, and said, "Give my love to Anne."

"Out! Delinquent."

John and I stood on my doorstep. He asked: "Anne? Or am I being nosy?"

"Yes, you are; but never mind. Anne is Dr Anne Holt, an anthropologist, Dad's lady friend."

"So Professor Hope has a distinguished girlfriend to match his distinction." I didn't reply to that. He said, "Sit in the back." I opened the door and slid on to the seat. Surprised, I saw that someone else was there.

"Hi, Dawn."

It was Diana Gilbert.

So why should I be surprised? The bloody woman seemed to follow me everywhere. And of course I should have remembered Commander Maddox, for that guy seemed to have his fingers in many pies. I glanced at Diana, and thought, *Of course!* She's the ideal person for what I suspected would be a lot of running around damp fields, climbing rocky hills, and peering through night glasses for hours on end, and getting soaked and a head cold. Oh, yes, Diana the Huntress – in her home territory, Norfolk, the Broads, windswept beaches, and the freezing North Sea. She probably skinny-dipped in it. What a strange mixture–the sybarite and the judo fighter!

I felt we were going to be in for a rough weekend, so I lay back and closed my eyes. But that didn't last long, especially for someone like me, who also had two sides to my character: the intellectual and the sybarite. OK: I played fast netball, but that was in civilised surroundings, with a shower after a game, followed by a frosted glass of white wine.

My worst fears, as they say, were confirmed. We – about thirty of us, of both sexes – were housed in old corrugated barracks left over from WWII, fitted out with iron bedsteads and a blanket, one pillow (no sheets!) and a rusty locker. At least males and females were separated. I couldn't help noticing that my fellow 'prisoners' were all much younger – college grads? We were woken at six each morning and had to run round the perimeter, followed by horrible dark stewed tea and a greasy bacon sandwich.

We were kept so occupied with law lectures and what they politely termed 'field exercises', which meant, as I suspected, getting wet and muddied and cold, that we fell exhausted into our bunks before ten at night.

Carlo, where are you?

Chapter Nine

London: Milan

Looking through the open curtains at my bedroom window, I could see, across the edge of the park, that overnight the summer was ending. The start of the day was noticeably cooler. The skyline had shadows of grey across the pale yellow horizon, increasing almost as I watched. I shivered, closed the small upper window and drew the curtains closer. Was September going to be an arbiter of my life change? But I first had more immediate things to do, such as finding a warm dressing-gown and making my father's early-morning cup of tea. That was the time when I sat on the edge of his bed and we discussed the plans (or not) for the day. He said:

"You say first. And no frivolous remarks, child."

"Of course not, Pops. Well... I have work to do for the Agency this morning, then I'm meeting Diana for lunch – a business lunch, no less."

"I've heard of those gatherings; there seems to be more lunch than business."

"Don't you believe it! You would be appalled at the lack, or quality, of food I've attended in the past."

"Continue, please."

I took a swallow of the rich brown tea. "Actually, father, in all seriousness, this could be a major breach of import regulations, with serious criminal proceedings."

"What! It sounds terrifying. I don't suppose you are allowed to discuss it."

"You are right: it is not even official yet. That's why I need to talk with Diana."

"Understood."

"By the way. What are you up to? C'mon: tell all."

"I shall be working on the Codex all morning. Then, like you, I shall be out to lunch."

"With Anne? Business lunch at the college?"

"Very amusing, Dawn. As a matter of fact we are meeting at the Faculty."

"The food there is awful. I recommend Prezzo round the corner. By the way, Father…"

"Yes…"

"I just wanted to let you know that I think it's lovely that you two have got together."

"Oh, well. Thank you."

Then the next thing I did when returned to my room was to open my laptop, and check my emails. Nothing from Carlo. Hmm. This morning was not the day for a tarty Armani suit and killer heels, but a respectable wool dress. I finished Frances's Italian translation by late morning, locked them in my briefcase, and remembered to rescue my new Customs ID. As I was leaving the house, Anne's car drew up. She slipped out of the driver's seat – a sprightly, elegant, elderly lady.

"Hello, Anne."

"Dawn – nice to see you. Are you well?"

"Thank you, yes. And you?"

"Fine. I'm taking your father to the Faculty – saves him trailing all over London."

After those formalities were over, I said, "I have to rush. Meeting. Have a nice lunch." I wanted to get away before she started asking about my father; why, I didn't know. And also before she offered me a lift. Why the reluctance? I didn't know that, either. Well, actually I did: I was uncertain about their relationship. I was shocked at myself, realising that I might be jealous. *Oh, for goodness' sake, Dawn – grow up.*

This grumble partly had its roots in that, in hoping to kick-start an investigation, Carlo had not replied to my email. I tried to get to Frances's office as quickly as possible, arriving at the Agency a bit hot and bothered, with my silk vest sticking to my back. I slung my jacket over the back of the chair at my usual desk then stuck my head round Frances's door. "Work all done, Frances; where do you wish it?"

She looked over her half-moon specs and pointed a finger at her desk. She said,

"And good afternoon to you, 007. Do you have a meeting at Thames House?"

"Very funny, Mrs Brooke. No: lunch with Mrs Gilbert – Department business."

Frances smiled. "Where? The Civil Service canteen?"

"Hardly. Fifth floor, Harvey Nicks."

"Why am I not surprised?"

"Why do you say that, Frances?"

She gave me an old-fashioned look, then waved me away. "As long as you don't expect the Department to pay for it."

"Chance would be a fine thing."

As I entered the swish cafe with the glass roof at Harvey Nichols, I spotted Diana immediately and waved; she grinned at me. She had nabbed a table overlooking Sloane Square. Diana was wearing a suit-jacket and pencil skirt, in some sort of purple fabric; underneath, a silk blouse straining against her bosom. She kissed me on the cheek, then said:

"So, what is all the mystery?"

"Get me a lemon spritzer, then I'll tell you." She beckoned to a waitress. I opened my briefcase, then halted; I touched her wrist with my hand. Diana frowned.

I asked, "By the way, have you got one of these?" I opened the ID and waved it. She delved into her own bag, then we both giggled. I said:

"You realise, Mata Hari, that we can just stroll in anywhere by flashing these – banks, bonded warehouses, foreign trucks…"

"I used to gain entrance by flashing my tits."

"Behave: we are now officials of H.M.G. And act accordingly. Anyway, never mind that; we'll finish this smoked salmon, then I'll explain this mysterious encounter."

"Aren't we allowed a glass of white wine?"

"Certainly not – this is business. That is why we are not dining in the main restaurant; elderly ladies go there to be seen. Here is more discreet."

"I didn't realise that you could be such a bossy-boots."

"You ain't seen nothin' yet."

We finished the brunch meal in silence, drinking only water. The waitress cleared the plates, then brought coffee.

"So," said Diana, "come clean."

I explained how I talked my way into Carlo's apartment block in Mayfair, and what I found on his computer. Diana – the print-outs on her knees – glanced through the notes that Carlo had made on his son Aldo's movements. She slid them back into my document case.

"So," I asked, "what do you think?"

"What am I supposed to think? All I know about the man is the little you've told me. And why is he so worried about his son's movements? And what have these so-called 'lost' paintings to do with it – if anything?"

"Surely, isn't it obvious – pages of reproductions of stolen paintings…"

"…Which are available to anybody with a PC."

"Followed by all the reports on Aldo's movements – Rome, Milan, Venice. Well, I believe there is." I wasn't too pleased by the doubt on Diana's face. She said:

"Look, Dawn: there is only a strong suspicion that boy Aldo is up to some funny business; but you have no actual proof."

"Then we get some."

"Oh, it's 'we', is it? What makes you think I want to get involved in all this?"

That took me back: I never considered that Diana wouldn't want to help me.

"Look, Dawn: just consider one thing. Are you sure that your judgement is not being coloured by the fact that you haven't seen Carlo in months; and you might want to? So this so-called case you've built up in your mind is an excuse?"

I felt myself blushing hard; I was suddenly very angry. "Certainly not! How can you say that, Diana?"

"All I'm say, kiddo, is think about it calmly. Think. That is what academics are supposed to be good at." I calmed down a little, but was still feeling stubborn; and I didn't like that snide remarks about academics. Diana said:

"Don't pout, Dawn. Look: if we can find a link, however tenuous, I'll help you. Why don't you come over to Pimlico and let Max have his say." So I agreed to that.

I realised that I was behaving impetuously. It was now a matter of swallowing my pride, and acting sensibly. Anyhow, we took the Tube from Sloane Square to Victoria and changed trains to Pimlico. As we walked to Diana's house. I said, "Will Max be home?"

"I should think so; but there wouldn't be much point in phoning: he never answers while he's working."

The house seemed empty, and I said so. "Oh, no: Max'll be in the studio. I'll get him." She ran upstairs. But something caught my eye as I wandered into the sitting-room. I leaned over the sofa: it was Max; he was asleep. He had a cushion under his head, his arms folded across his stomach; he looked as peaceful as a child. His long features were smooth, except for incipient bulges under his eyes. His hair, swept back from his forehead, was still dark, with touches of grey at the temples; his forehead was practically unlined: a distinguished man. I stood quietly and put my finger to my lips as Diana entered the room. I whispered, "Max is asleep."

"No, I am not. You have interrupted my time for deep thought."

Diana leaned over her husband and kissed his forehead. "Rubbish. It was no such thing; you were having your post-prandial nap. Wakey-wakey, darling, we need your expertise." She looked at me. "Dawn: give my lazy husband a resume while I boil a kettle."

Diana made a large pot of coffee and I spread the sheets from the printer across the kitchen table.

"So," said Max, "what do we have? I see pages written in Italian with dates at their heading; presumably some sort of diary? And reproductions of paintings which are no longer on public – or even private – view. Presumably because they were lost or stolen?"

"Correct, Max," I said.

"So what is the connection between the diary sheets and the paintings?"

I explained how I had 'retrieved' the information from Carlo's computer; about his wayward son Aldo; and how I put two and two together – and possibly come up with five. I realised suddenly that what I had called 'evidence' was just an assumption.

Max frowned. "Do you realise that there are thousands of missing paintings – important works from hundreds of years – that will never be seen again? I ask myself once more, Dawn – why these?"

Diana said: "From what Dawn has said about her lover's–" (I winced) "son, there'll be some funny business with loads of cash for little Aldo."

Her husband replied: "Well first of all let me look at the paintings and put them into some sort of sequence – dates, of course, and provenance."

So Max (although I don't know why I was surprised at his efficiency) opened a large notebook and started to place the works of art in their chronological sequence, starting of course with their known date of execution; if not certain, he put a question mark against a date. Then, in a second column, he put the estimated date of their loss. Of course, I had done some of the groundwork by attacking Carlo's computer and printing off the results. I thought all this was rather tedious and unnecessary; but I could hardly complain: I was consulting one of England's most distinguished artists. All this, I appreciated, was needed for Max to allow his instinct to come to some sort of conclusion – or at least to guesstimate which painting had the best chance of being recovered or discovered.

Eventually, he said: "Well, from the list we have here there is no doubt about their provenance. They are comprehensively documented. Now: pay attention, ladies! First, the Vermeer, stolen from the Isabella Stewart Gardner Museum in 1990, entitled *The Concert*. It has never been recovered – but what a find!" He frowned. "But, no: I can't see that being hawked around Europe – I doubt even the dubious Eastern oligarchs would touch it."

Max went through the list with similar thoroughness: *The Just Judges* (Van Eyck), which was stolen – as part of an altarpiece in Ghent – in 1934 (Max considered that because the thief refused to name its whereabouts even on his deathbed it was probably destroyed); a Rubens (*Judith Beheading Holofernes*); and one Raphael.

But Max was of the opinion that the likeliest candidate was another Raphael – *Portrait of a Young Man*, called Bembo. There was a problem with the history of this work: it was said to have been stolen by the Nazi governor-general in Poland, Hans Frank, for Goering's private collection. (The Americans caught up with Frank in Bavaria; he was shot in the leg.) Reproductions of the painting show the young man looking at the viewer out of the corner of his eyes; his features are rather feminine. But the truth of the matter is that it is in the collection of the Szepmuveszefi Museum in Budapest. Max didn't know that: it was just as well that I double-checked my sources.

After about an hour of this back-and-froing Diana said: "Well, Max, what do you think? Is Dawn on to something?"

Max frowned again, then said: "In my opinion if any of these works are in the possession of Aldo it would be the Van Eycks' altarpiece; although considered opinion is that it was eventually destroyed."

He threw up his arms. "But who knows!"

We all sat quietly, thinking, for a few minutes. Eventually, I said:

"Well, this all speculation. Let's just put it all in front of Maddox, and see what he thinks. It might just come to nothing, Diana." I turned to Max. "May I quote you, Max?"

He laughed. "I doubt whether it will do you much good, Dawn. Now: may I return to my studio?"

"Oh, yes; sorry. We've taken you away from your work…"

Diana said: "That's a major crime in this household," then kissed her husband on both cheeks. I suddenly felt a surge of envy – then guilt for such an irrational thought. (*Carlo, where are you?*)

I hurried home after leaving Max to his painting and Diana to whatever she did. My father was still out. First thing: check my emails. I flipped open my laptop: there was one message: from Carlo, timed 30 minutes previously. It said:

Please stay by your email and cell-phone. I need your help. Then please follow my instructions. Immediately. Trust me. I still love you. Carlo.

Now this was too much of a coincidence. Was it about my suspicions of his wayward son? Or was it something completely different, and had nothing to do with Aldo? Carlo had asked me to help him – stay by my phone. So I did. And a lot longer than I expected – where had the urgency in his message gone? An hour seemed an age; but it gave me an unwanted opportunity to wonder what was really happening in Carlo's world. As soon as I had read his email, I checked my cell-phone; nothing there in the intervening half-hour.

While I was waiting, I thought, *What do I really know about Carlo Palladio?* I knew, of course, that he was married to this grande dame of an old Italian family (I wonder how much deft negotiation had gone on behind the scenes before they walked down the aisle?); that his other son, Ricardo, was a financial director of one of his father's firms – married with two children. His daughter, Clara, was married to some useless Venetian Count; they had a son: so he had at least done his duty there. That was Carlo's family. Nobody knew him (I liked to think) more fleshly, more intimately, than I. Of course I had seen him in action during a business meeting: that was impressive, the way he could hold several different facts in his head at once and produce them quickly. I don't think anyone could pull a fast one on Carlo.

So perhaps I didn't need to know any more. Except of course with the – to my mind – silly idea of his becoming a Euro MP, and chumming up with Berlusconi!

Then my cell phone rang

"Carlo?!"

"Si, Dawn. You are at home?"

"Yes. Carlo, are you all right? What's happened?"

"I need your help, *cara*."

"So you said – what do you want me to do?"

"Will you do as I ask, and trust me?"

I hesitated, just for a moment. "Yes, Carlo. You know I will."

"Then please listen carefully."

I was just leaving home, a travel bag in the hallway, unlocking the front door, when my father and Anne walked up the steps; he was leaning on her arm. My father said:

"Oh, hullo, where are you off to, Dawn?"

Anne shot quick glances at us both. "Are you all right, Dawn?"

"Yes, thanks, Anne. Look: I have to be away for a few days. Department business. I can't say where, but I'll be in touch regularly. OK?"

My father looked alarmed. "If you say so. Will Diana be with you?"

"Later on." I picked up my bag as the car drew up. I kissed my father. "Look after him, Anne."

"Of course. And you be very careful."

As I sat in the back of the Merc, I tried to think if he was the driver who had collected me all that time ago when I had my first assignation with Carlo. I tried to make out his features but nothing registered.

Will Diana be with you? My father had asked. *No. Nobody will be with me, Dad.*

Breaking rules, I had advised no one. I looked again at my driver: he didn't look round at me or at his mirror: he just drove purposefully. And he drove quickly for the short journey, zipping to a halt outside Paddington Underground. He opened my door, then passed me an envelope.

"What's this?" I asked.

He didn't look at me, a featureless, broad-shouldered man in a dark-blue suit and crisp white shirt who just kept glancing around. He said: "Tube ticket to Heathrow, Miss. Then go straight to terminal 4. Have a safe journey. All is arranged."

I protested: "Why not take me all the way to the airport, then?"

"Those are my instructions, Miss."

So I would have to change at Earls Court to the Piccadilly Line, which was a bore. If I was lucky, the journey to Heathrow would be under 50 minutes. Then what would happen? I didn't even know where I was going. What did I have – clothes in a large grip; passport and my Customs ID in a secret pocket on my shoulder bag. As I sat in the crowded carriage – cluttered of course with air travellers' hefty, hazardous baggage – I thought, *Dawn, what are you letting yourself in for?* I looked round. A young swarthy man bumped his case against my trouser leg. He looked, down, and shrugged as he glanced at me. I read his luggage label, and spoke to him in his own language (French).

"Don't shrug your shoulders at me, my friend. Just look where you're going!"

He was startled and held up a hand. "Pardon, madame."

I don't know why I became a linguist. I don't like the rude French, the proud Spanish, the stiff Germans. But then there are the Italians. Ahh, the Italians… such an intensely irritating people at times. But could I live in Italy? Oh, yes: it was the only place I could live outside England.

Most of the passengers in my compartment got out at the terminal 3 stop; I was able to stretch my legs then stand in comfort. I looked up at an advertisement opposite me. It wanted us all to holiday in the Seychelles; really? Well, chance would be a fine thing.

I took a seat in a corner of the reception area, and read the remainder of the envelope's contents. Enclosed was a business-class ticket, BA, London-Milan (one way. Why one way?!) and five 100 Euro notes that looked as though they had just been printed; I rubbed them between my thumb and finger: they had a soft, silky feel, like a Dior fabric. A bribe, Carlo – or just running expenses? There was a note, printed out from a computer in Times Roman capitals. TAKE THE LATE FLIGHT TO MILAN, MALPENSA AIRPORT. THEN EXPRESS TRAIN TO CITY CENTRE. MY ASSOCIATE HELENA WILL MEET YOU. SHE WILL IDENTIFY HERSELF. C.

Well, well, all very mysterious. And who was Helena? The train from the airport should take about 40 minutes. That would bring me into Milan at… I looked up at the VDU; time to board.

Sitting by a port-side window as the plane swept skywards (a sudden splash of silver light across the grey swell of the Thames), I thought why Carlo had instructed people to take me, by car, only as far as the Tube station; and also nobody meeting me at Milan airport. Why? Because at rail stations nobody takes any notice of anyone else; they're too busy running for trains with their heads down. But at airports, there were always people sat around waiting the interminable hour before boarding, reading newspapers or blinking at laptops, or just staring into space. And there was always someone watching with a purpose; and I don't mean a couple of uniformed police constables with machine pistols. The authorities have plain-clothes people all over the building watching every movement of the various crowds queuing to show passports and standing (patiently) for security checks.

Was that why Carlo had inconvenienced me? Or was I getting paranoid? *No, Dawn: you didn't think of that all by your little self; you thought it because that was one of the things they had taught you.*

But before I could think of any more smart moves, the chief steward announced out approach to Malpensa; people began to stir; businessmen closed their briefcases and laptops. I'd heard it was definitely cooler in Milan, so I had brought my belted wool jacket with the faux fur collar to wear over my (rather thin Armani) suit jacket (vanity, vanity!); I also had a wool hat and leather gloves. I climbed out of the express train at Stazione Nord – ironically, more city-central than the Centrale station.

As I walked, I kept well away from the platform and let the crowds rush past me. And then I spotted her.

She was of medium height, wearing slim, dark, ski-like pants; a deep-red roll-neck sweater; over that, a short leather jack. So this, hopefully, was Helena – Helena what? I should say that Helena was in her early forties. Her hair was a dense, although shiny black, cut page-boy style; wide-set brown eyes; heart-shaped face. She smiled, and held out her hand.

"Signorina Hope?"

"Before I answer that, could you please prove who you are?"

Raised eyebrows, then a shrug. She dug into her shoulder bag, then showed me an identity card covered in clear plastic. It had her photo, name and a department in the Universita Degli Studi de Milano. She had spoken in English. I now replied in Italian. "Grazzi, Doctor Bolzano. Excuse the doubt, but…" I showed her my passport. "Now we know who we are," I continued, "what do you have to tell me?"

Doctor Bolzano was a lecturer at the medical post-graduate school in the university, and a cousin on Carlo's distaff side. We climbed into an insignificant FIAT, and she shot off and headed north. Eventually we reached the Duomo, continuing north at a suicidal pace. When I got my breath back I said:

"So, what is this all about – what does Carlo want that is so urgent? Why me?"

Helena said: "He said you were beautiful. He was right."

"Never mind my looks! Answer me."

"He needs a translation of a very obscure document. Some sort of ancient East European paper."

I was getting annoyed. I was also tired and hungry. "Then he may have come to the wrong person. By the way, where are we going?"

"Brera."

I might have known: Milan's trendy quarter (fashionable shops, bars, and expensive apartments), pretending to be New York's SoHo. I said, "Helena, you are not telling me everything. What else is there?"

She glanced quickly at me. "I honestly don't know, Dawn. I think politics is involved…"

"I hope Carlo hasn't got mixed up with Berlusconi's dirty business."

Helena didn't answer. But I persisted. "So, you live in Brera?"

"Yes."

"Will Carlo be there?"

"Yes. But please leave it there, OK?"

I had to be content with that. For the rest of the journey, I thought about how I began this narrative. Seeing Carlo in Nice, which now seemed such a long time ago at that awful, vulgar (and outrageously expensive) hotel; the beautiful clothes I wore; how I loved him; and how I put my feet on the path to betraying him. But now I had a strong feeling that I hadn't. He certainly sounded desperate. I should just have to wait and see.

Helena parked her Fiat in a cul-de-sac and we walked up a short hill in the dark to her apartment; I looked up from the narrow street at the tall block: along each balcony residents had planted pots full of geraniums that hid the windows. Behind each balcony, chinks of light peeped through the closed shutters; muffled sounds of peoples' voices leaked through as well. Helena unlocked the twin outside doors with a security card; it was dark in the hallway, but a light came on in the lift as she opened its doors. It was narrow and we were pressed disconcertingly together. She pressed a button for the fifth floor. "I live on the top floor," she said unnecessarily.

Her apartment door was opposite the lift. She searched in her bag for keys, but as soon as she inserted one in the lock, the door swung open, and Carlo stood in front of me, a light behind him. I was blinded for a moment; his dark shape looked like a phantom.

As soon as he saw me he said, huskily, "Dawn. Thank God!" Helena brushed past us and strode down the corridor.

We hugged each other, and I said, pushing him away, "Oh, Carlo – what have you been up to?" I felt like crying. He took my hand and led me down the darkened corridor, my heels clacking on the marble floor. We entered the living room; it was lit only by two sconce lights on each wall, and a huge table lamp on a large round smoked glass coffee table. There were two long sofas in pale leather. On the far wall the lighting illuminated a long tapestry, denoting (as usual) the medieval symbols of a young woman in a garden; opposite her a white unicorn, his twisted horn phallically thrusting from his forehead, pointing towards her. I gazed at Carlo, as if seeing him for the first time; he looked dreadful. The dapper billionaire seemed to have shrunk in his clothes; he had bags under his eyes like bruises.

I asked him again. "Carlo: What the hell has been happening?" A wave of tiredness ran through me. Helena had just removed herself to one of the sofas saying nothing. I was getting fed up with this. "Now look," I said, "you've dragged me half way across Europe at a moment's notice. I am tired, cold and hungry. So while you two gather your thoughts in a logical manner I'm going to take a shower and change. And when I come out, I expect a hot meal and a decent bottle of wine. Is that OK?"

Helena said, "I don't keep much here, Diana…"

"Well don't you think you should have thought of that? Isn't there a trattoria near here?"

His cousin looked as although she was going to give me an argument. (How long had she had to put up with Carlo in her home?) But Carlo said, "Please, Helena; do as Dawn asks."

So I took myself off to the bathroom. After my shower, I phoned my father and reassured him. When I emerged, in silk pyjamas and kimono (so easy to roll into a small bundle for packing), but still drying my hair, Carlo was lying full length on one of the sofa. I leaned over and kissed him. I said "Are you awake, *cara*?"

He just smiled, then said: "Thank you for coming, Dawn."

'When we've eaten – and you look as though you've not had a proper meal in days – you can tell me what the hell is going on. Where's Helena?"

As if summoned, I heard the front door slam open; she came through and placed boxes of food on the large coffee table and a bottle of valpolicella. She said, "OK, so there's your food. I'm leaving now, driving to my cottage at Como."

She looked really fed up. Carlo said: "Very well, Helena. And thank you for everything."

She shrugged. "Just phone me when you've finished. I expect to see my apartment empty when I return." She collected her bag, and turned on her heel. She didn't say anything to me.

I said, "I don't think your cousin likes me."

Carlo gave a grim smile. "Nor me, Dawn. I've been here for the past week. I've invaded her home."

After our (fairly) hot meal I pushed the plates away and poured more wine; Carlo now looked more human; the wine had put colour in his cheeks. I said:

"Why Helena?"

"She and my security staff are the only ones I can trust."

"She's a doctor? A physician?' Is she married?" I didn't want some husband barging in while I was here.

Carlo shook his head. "Helen lectures at the postgraduate medical school. She is devoted to her profession. No: there is no husband."

"OK, Carlo: what's this all about? Are you in trouble? And what about this East European document?"

As I suspected, it was politics. And, as I was to learn, murky dealings with Berlusconi at the centre of it. Literally. The old roué had had been caught on camera with his pants down. Yes: photographic evidence, and I was staring at it: a black-and-white 10 by 8 glossy nude picture of old 'Bunga Bunga' himself on his back with a naked busty blonde astride him. There were others (different positions). But all of him – and with different girls. Carlo slid the photos swiftly back into the manila envelope; he looked very uncomfortable; in fact, he seemed ashamed that he was involving me in the dirty business.

I said: "Carlo, why have you brought me here? Sure, all the world knows that your pal screws around. Now there are photos. What is this – blackmail?"

What it all amounted to was this: Whoever it was had taken the photographs had demanded serious money for their return. "How much?" I asked Carlo.

"One million euros."

"Is that all? His organisation could pay that and not miss it. "But why have you got the photos, Carlo?"

"I negotiated a deal with the Party. If I can resolve this without anybody knowing, my status would go through the roof. It is, as you say, a quid quo pro."

So, Carlo would realise his ambitions of being a big player on the European political stage just by washing Berlusconi's dirty linen in secret. I just could not understand why Carlo should wish to agree to all this. Hadn't he got everything in life that any man could wish? But no: I should have known; my lover never stood still. I said:

"Who else knows about this? Your wife, for example?"

"Maria? No!"

"Your children?"

"Only Aldo. He has been my eyes and ears. Plus three men from my security staff; they are discreet, unobtrusive, and follow orders. When Aldo wasn't collecting the photos one of my other men were."

Of course, that was the reason why Carlo had Aldo's movements logged day by day. But where did the paintings come into this? I thought I'd leave that for now. I said: "Now what about this document?" Carlo told me that when one photo had been received, there was a simple note:

There are more like these. We require one million euros for the remainder. Await instructions.

Carlo had been summoned to Rome and advised of the unexploded bomb. He had agreed to handle negotiations. So he took Aldo into his confidence. Brief notes kept arriving, with instructions to go to certain places and wait. And every time Aldo arrived at, say, Padua, there would be another note and another photograph. These people were playing with Berlusconi and his pals, having Aldo and the others running round northern Italy. No wonder Carlo was a nervous wreck. The last photograph in an envelope also contained the mysterious document.

I asked: "Where did Aldo have to collect this?"

"The Duomo."

"The Duomo! Why on earth there? And where is Aldo now?"

"I told him to lose himself. He's probably taken his girlfriend to Genoa. He has a small boat in the harbour; they both like sailing. I want him out of the way, Dawn."

"Very sensible. Look: does Helena have an office, a study?"

"Yes, through here." It was part of the guest bedroom; a desk placed against the window, overlooking the narrow street. It was clear of papers; just a desk lamp. I sat down and drew the desk lamp towards me, switched it on and held the document to the light. Carlo peered over my shoulder. He said, "It looks very old."

"That's what you were meant to think. Look," I said, "can you see the watermark?"

"Yes."

"It says 'Fabriano', with code letters. This so-called parchment could have been purchased at any art materials store within the last year."

"Dawn! How clever of you to know that."

Yes, well: I'm not my father's daughter for nothing.

"That's what you were meant to think."

"What do you mean?"

I couldn't do this with Carlo constantly at my shoulder. I said, "Carlo, why don't you go to bed? You look all in. I'll work on this for an hour. Before that make us a large pot of coffee. OK?" Carlo did as he was bid. I could hear him in the kitchen washing dishes. Good boy. The first line of the 'ancient' document was written in what I first thought was Russian (why Russian?) but it didn't make sense; there was no grammar. Then it dawned on me that the letters weren't Cyrillic script: they were Church Slavonic – the language adopted by Eastern Orthodox Church for its liturgy. Now: could I do a transliteration? The trouble was, of course, that these eastern languages such as Latvian, Lithuanian, Estonian (under the generic term Uralic), had pinched bits from each other over the centuries.

I decided that it would be a waste of time trying to work at an exact translation; what was required was a rough approximation; these people weren't writing a scholarly thesis: they wanted to get their message across. But I also suspected there was a moral dig; they wanted to punish Berlusconi. So there was no point in fooling around with Runic alphabets. After some jigging around, with similar characters in both Russian and Slavonic, I came up with the following, in capitals:

THE WAGES OF SIN IS DEATH

Crikey! What was all this about? If we were going to have quotes from the Bible, what next? The text that followed was irritating and a damn nuisance: it was though the sender was deliberately trying to annoy me. It was mainly in Latin; but all sorts of characters were thrown in – a tiresome mixture of Greek (*Dad, where are you?*) Church Coptic and Cyrillic; the similarities between the two languages of course was another sting in the tail. At least there were no fiddly diacritic accents, such as acutes, lenis, circumflex etc. Well – whoever you are – if you think I'm going to be stymied by mixing Russian and Coptic, you've got another think coming; that's far too easy.

The whole thing was a process of elimination. Then I glanced at my watch; I was dreadfully tired. Enough for one night: it was past midnight. Time for bed. But I was not going anywhere near Carlo. I looked in the main bedroom and he was fast asleep; the sound of his deep breathing reached my hearing as I opened the door. I closed it behind me.

I made myself comfortable in the spare bedroom (where the desk and my notes were situated) and hugged myself under Helena's duvet. All I needed was a glass of water. The practical thing about silk pyjamas was that they are so warm in climates like northern Italy, when the cool winds in autumn blow across the lake from Como and the mountains to Milan. I also wore wool socks; why the Italians insist on always having marble floors beats me. (Historical and irrelevant note: During the First World War, British soldiers tried to get their mothers and wives to send them long silk drawers to wear in the trenches in the winter.)

I fell asleep immediately.

The next thing I knew was Carlo bending over me with a cup of coffee. I blinked over the duvet. "*Boungiorno, cara.*"

"And good morning to you, Carlo. What's the time?"

"Nine a.m., and a beautiful day." Carlo looked like his old dapper self, and more than half human. I said so. He smiled. "Your presence, darling, makes everything right."

I said: "Really? Well, scoot while I make myself decent. And I'll have fresh rolls for breakfast."

While I was chewing on a roll I thought of the time I downloaded Carlo's computer when we were in Nice. Our assumptions then were way out; we thought Carlo's son Aldo had nicked 'lost' paintings and was trying to flog them to the Russians. Had I got that completely wrong? But what else was I going to think? What was actually going on was Aldo reporting to his father on the trail of dirty photos of Berlusconi. But I still thought that there was some connection with the paintings. And also what I had translated so far in that phony 'document'. I mean, why go to all that trouble? I was still thinking along those lines when I put further work on it during the morning. About 11 a.m. I called Carlo in; my eyes were aching and I had a pain in my neck – which was exactly what I thought the document was.

Carlo came into the room, all eager. He said: "You have finished? What does it say?"

"I'm going to disappoint you, my sweet."

"What do you mean! There is nothing?"

"Oh, there is plenty, all right. But not what you'd expect. All it is is a sermon, in biblical language, warning you about breaking the Commandments; sins of the flesh; and 'a man is judged by the company he keeps'. There is one thing for sure: it may be a nutcase who wrote this – but they know exactly what you've been doing for your pal."

"Yes, yes: we have the photographs.

"Carlo – think. Who would want to do this. Fanatical enough to behave like a religious maniac. Do you have enemies in the Church?"

"No, no. I have always had good relations with them. Maria, my wife, is very devout; I support the Church's charities generously."

"Hmmm. Well somebody's got it in not only for Berlusconi, but for you. Now, Carlo. When Aldo was instructed to collect the other photographs. Was it during the day or at night?"

"The late evening. They were always left in a church. He collected the packet; further instructions were with the photographs."

"Did he have to leave money?"

Carlo shook his head. "No money was demanded until the last package."

"And when will that be, Carlo?"

He handed me a package. "Tomorrow."

"When did this package arrive?"

"It was dropped through the letterbox at five a.m. this morning by one of my security men. It woke me."

Carlo had tried to reseal it, so I opened it with a paper knife that was on Helena's desk, and pulled out the contents. But there no photos of Berlusconi or fat blondes at *le moment critique*. Just one postcard with several views of Santa Maria Nascente: in other words Milan's Duomo, the sort of thing tourists bought. Well, if the naughty photos of Carlo's pal were published in next month's *Oggi* magazine it wouldn't be only St Maria ascending.

Well, well.

Carlo said, "Dawn? Dawn? Why are you smiling?"

"Mmm? Oh, sorry. They say you have to bring the money now – on the final collection?"

"Yes."

"Do you have that sort of money – here?"

"God, no."

"Well, I don't think you'll need it, darling."

"Why? Why not? What's going on?"

I stood away from the desk. 'Because, my sweet. This is not about blackmail – somebody's on a crusade. The money's just a blind. And you and Berlusconi are targets. Don't you see the pattern? All the collections were at churches in the evening, dark places. God: one would think it was like some distorted pilgrimage."

Carlo was now obviously agitated. "So what can I do except…"

"Except follow this to its conclusion, Carlo." I then made a decision. I had no choice. I couldn't leave him on his own. We would have to follow instructions to the letter. (And there wouldn't be much point in trying to hide his security thugs in such a massive edifice, but…) Carlo was now staring out of the window at the alley below.

I said: "Carlo: I'm coming with you."

I had startled him. "No! No, Dawn: I can't allow that."

I grasped him by the shoulders. "Oh, yes I am sweetie. You can hardly stop me. I have an idea. Will you trust me?"

"Of course." Well, he could hardly say anything else, could he? Trust works both ways.

We cleared the apartment; washed all the dishes, left the tiny kitchen immaculate. I remade the beds. By the time we closed the door behind us Helena would have no complaints. It was now dark on that evening as we walked down the narrow sloping street to the small piazza below. There was no illumination apart from slivers of light from apartment windows above our heads. The car that was waiting wasn't the usual black Merc; just a grey Fiat four-door saloon. But the man stood next to it wore a dark suit, white shirt, and black tie. He never stopped looking around as we approached.

"Who's this, Carlo?"

"One of my security staff."

"He looks like Mafia hit-man."

"Certainly not! All my staff are professional experts in investigating industrial espionage." (But I suspect that the principle of *omerta* applied.)

"Did they agree to my suggestion?"

"They did as I ordered, Dawn." So my name didn't come into it – fair enough.

Carlo spoke again, this time to our driver. "You know where we are going?"

"Of course, sir, and our positions when we arrive."

I just wanted get out of Brera, find the hotel, and be on my own. But Carlo, with his usual efficiency, had made arrangements for me to stay at the Sparadi – within walking distance of the Duomo at the corner of the piazza. They must know him very well, for the manager met me at the long desk with two of his staff – a porter and a young, dark-haired woman. He asked, "Signorina Hope? Everything is prepared. You can be assured that you will not be disturbed. Please telephone from your suite for any requirements."

"Grazi, senore."

The porter carried my overnight bag; the young woman (from reception) just walked behind me. She pushed open the double doors, then took my case from the porter. I tipped him and he left. She said, "Would you wish me to unpack. Signorina Hope?" I was looking round the room, which was a tribute to contemporary art-deco – minimalist, again. But it looked very comfortable. I was more interested in the view from the window: it looked straight across to the Duomo. Good.

I replied to her question: "No, thank you. But could you return in thirty minutes, please? I may need some things."

"Of course."

I unpacked my small bag, pyjamas under the pillow; blouses and smalls in a laundry bag provided by the hotel. My travelling coat I hung in a wardrobe. I stripped off my clothes and took a shower, then wrapped one of the hotel's fluffy white robes around me. Exactly half an hour later, the internal phone rang. "Prego."

"It is Sophia at Reception, Signorina."

"Please come up, Sophia."

She had a notepad and pen as she entered the room. "What can I get you, signorina?"

"First: copies of *Corriere del a Sera, La Stampa, Milano Finanza* and a copy of the *International Herald Tribune*. I'll also require a track suit in dark blue (no other markings), a pair of trainers, also in dark blue or black. I need some cotton underwear (Sloggi brand); three pairs of panties; two sports bras. I've written down the sizes for all of them. Is that OK?"

If Sophia thought this was a strange shopping list she didn't say so. I looked at her while she wrote all this down. She was about five-foot-eight in her heels, slim figure, wearing the usual uniform of a two-piece suit with a jacket and pencil-slim skirt; under the jacket she wore a white silk blouse. Sophia was a good-looking woman with what I called a 'Venetian face', with that bump at the top of her nose that the Italians call a 'Doge's nose' (see the portrait by Bellini of Loredan in the National Gallery, London).

She looked up at me and flashed a smile. "Will that be all?"

"Yes, thank you. I hope that is not too much trouble?"

"Of course not, Miss Hope!" She took my laundry bag away with her, and wished me good night; her English was impeccable. Now I had to think – but not on an empty stomach. I rang for room service and ordered a platter of seafood and a bottle of their best rose wine. After all, Carlo was paying. Whenever I pack my bag for an assignment in Europe, usually with business people (CEOs, company secretaries, etc.), I always include a pair of Zeiss mini-binoculars and a strong flashlight. One usually landed at major cities; but being met by my bosses' opposite numbers usually meant a long drive to some tacky (if newly built) industrial complex. And if you are the only woman in the delegation it is wise on the first evening to check the environs from a darkened hotel bedroom: hence the binoculars. I made it a policy never to dine with the men at the meeting; but always ate in my room. I was expected to join a pre-dinner drinks bash and circulate. That was part of my job. But then I would make myself scarce.

I slept well that night, not even thinking of the bizarre situation in which I found myself – or even dreaming about Carlo. They had left the newspapers I had ordered and the clean laundry outside the room, so I phoned room service for breakfast and took my time reading them, looking for any news – however minor – of Berlusconi.

There was no mention in the *Corriere* or *La Stampa*. The Italians are great scandalmongers; but perhaps they were tiring of Berlusconi and his antics; I know I was. In the *Milano Finanza*, there was a paragraph about his TV companies; but you could almost feel the reporter's shrug when he wrote that Berlusconi's behaviour had not affected the share value of his companies. I had just come out of the shower when the phone buzzed. It was my friend Sophia.

"Buongiorno, signorina."

"Good morning, Sophia."

"I have the items you ordered, Miss Hope."

"Oh, good, Could you bring them up, please?"

Five minutes later there was a knock on my door; I was still wearing the white robe: it was 11 a.m. If Sophie was surprised, she didn't show it. The dark-blue track suit was of a soft woollen material; the trainers, Nike. The underwear was in a plastic folder. Sophia showed me receipts, waited till I checked them, then passed me the change: 125 euros: I handed it back to her.

"But, signorina…?"

"You've earned it. Thanks, Sophia."

Delighted, blushing, she thanked me and left. Getting dressed, I realised that I had neglected something. I called my father on my cell-phone. He said, "Where are you, Dawn?"

"Milan."

"What on earth are you doing there?'

"Not for pleasure, I can assure you. Is everything OK at home?"

"Perfectly. I am working, then out for lunch. By the way, it is raining here."

"Well, here it's cold but fine. Having lunch with Anne?"

"No. As a matter of fact with your colleague John Hibbert."

"Oh really. How come?"

"He invited me to Scotland Yard. I accepted."

We said our goodbyes, and I switched off. John Hibbert! At Scotland Yard! I was really put out. What was he playing at? I didn't trust him – was he trying to get round me through my father? I stopped. What on earth was I thinking? *Dawn Hope: you are getting paranoid.*

I dressed and tucked my new purchases away in my baggage. I needed to get out of this hotel room; I was feeling claustrophobic. It was cold walking across the piazza to the Duomo, and I appreciated my travelling coat and wool hat. There were the usual crowds of sightseers and chattering Italians, but no guides with their bright umbrellas waving, trying to herd their flocks of tourists. I stood back from the enormous cathedral with its innumerable spires like spears invading heaven, and thought, *This is one of the ugliest buildings I've ever seen*. Now, that would amount to blasphemy to any Milanese. Even with its tons of rose marble and awe-inspiring entrances, I kept asking myself, *what was it for?* Church services, obviously. But was it a monument to God, or a memorial to the city fathers? What it was meant to do of course was to inspire awe; to demonstrate the power of the Church. But I agreed with John Ruskin, that it was a mish-mash of different styles laid down without hardly any aesthetic continuance. But perhaps it was my Scandinavian Lutheran background coming through, and I wasn't here to form an artistic opinion.

I followed a few straggling tourists as they wandered through the brass doors. As I entered its gloomy interior, I could see down the centre of the church to the altar. We all stood for a while, then I left the group, because I noticed a small plaque denoting the entrance to a baptistery. I climbed the stairwell and looked around: I made sure that I remembered. I retraced my steps and made my way to the north side. There was a lift that would take me to the roof of the Duomo. No matter how cynical one was about this structure, the view from this height was breath-taking; I stood, transfixed. After a while I realised that I was cold and decided that I had had enough of this structure, so I left.

Joining Milan's fashionable society, I sat outside an elegant cafe in the Galleria Vittorio Emanuele and watched the world go by-and thought and thought. Finishing a latte and a sticky patisserie, I made my way back to the hotel; as I passed the reception, I asked about any messages: there was one, in a sealed envelope. I asked whether they knew who had left it: "No, signorina; just a man in a dark suit." That would be one of Carlo's hoods (I still think they looked like gangsters).

In my room, I tore open the envelope. It was from Carlo, of course:

The rendezvous is at 10 p.m. this evening at the west door of the Duomo. Please be outside your hotel at 9.30 p.m. I will have stationed six men at the Duomo as you suggested. All will be in radio contact with me.

I spent the remainder of the afternoon at the window with the binoculars. What was I hoping to see? During those hours I noticed nothing unusual. At 5 p.m. stewards were closing the great brass doors; I swept the facade of the great church with the binoculars for the next few hours: nothing doing. My eyes were feeling the strain, so I stripped off my shirt, silk briefs, bra and trousers, sluiced my face and chest, and changed into the cotton underwear and tracksuit and trainers, plus my coat with the fur collar. I packed all my discarded clothes into my case – and waited, baggage at my feet, flashlight in my coat pocket. At exactly 9:25 I descended the rear stairs, which had a notice saying 'STAFF ONLY', and found myself at the kitchen. Only one thing to do – dash right through. But none of the chefs seemed to notice.

I walked quickly across the piazza towards the Duomo. It was dark now, but that didn't help me, for the illumination had been switched on at the front of the cathedral. I had no choice except to head in a westerly direction. Eventually, I was able to move into the shadows of the building, and slowed to a strolling pace.

Shadows moved into the corner of my vision: two figures. Carlo said:

"Everything all right, Dawn?"

I passed my case to his companion. "Can you put this in your vehicle?" He moved away. I said to Carlo, "Everything's fine. Now: are you in radio contact with Franco and all your men?" He held up the walkie-talkie. "Just making sure, Carlo." I suddenly thought, *Why am I doing this? Acting like some character out of a second-rate TV spy thriller?*

I didn't ask how Carlo managed to obtain entrance to the building; when we got inside, the place echoed to our footsteps. I stood still, held Carlo's arm, and whispered in his ear, "Don't move; keep still." His arm trembled.

Gradually, our eyes got used to the gloom. So we made our way to the rendezvous point: it seemed to take ages. I was scared; scared for Carlo, scared for me – and scared of what we might find.

I gripped Carlo's arm tighter. Once again, we stood perfectly still. I flashed my torch quickly. The light caught the sign to the baptistery I had seen earlier. Then I pointed the torch to the marble floor. Suddenly, above our heads a light on one of the pillars came on; we jumped and stumbled back. Two figures stood about two metres away. Because of the light behind them they were just black shapes. One of them moved towards us and spoke.

"So, Carlo, you have brought your harlot with you!"

Carlo gripped my hand. "Maria! Is it you?"

His wife came closer. She was dressed entirely in black. I flashed my torch on her and we could now see her clearly. In both hands she held a brass crucifix above her head. She moved threateningly towards her husband.

Carlo said: "Dear God, Maria: what are you doing? Are you mad?"

During this, I was watching the other person – a man in a monk's habit with a hood. He stood perfectly still. He shook his head and his hood fell back showing a white lining; his bearded face glared at me. That's all we needed: a Dominican. Suddenly, he opened his sleeve and scattered sheets of white paper in front of us – more photographs; photos of Berlusconi. Maria shouted:

"Carlo, you have brought shame on our family with this filth. Trying to hide from the face of God this man's depravity. But God sees everything!"

So we were faced with two religious fanatics. This is what we had come to; no political rivals; no criminals. Carlo was rooted to the floor, unable to believe his eyes; it was like a nightmare.

The Dominican said to me, "Beg forgiveness, whore. On your knees!' Did he really think I was one of Berlusconi's tarts?

Maria darted forward, aiming the heavy cross at Carlo's head. Then she seemed to freeze, her body bent backwards, and her feet suddenly swept away from her. She spun off the ground, the crucifix fell from her hands and clattered on the marble floor. As she hit the ground, her head struck the corner of a pillar and she groaned quietly.

I said to Diana: "What am I supposed to say – 'You took your time'?"

Diana moved swiftly towards the woman's body; but she was stopped as the Dominican flung his arm around her throat, attempting to pull her away. Diana dropped to her knees and pulled him over her shoulder; he flew on to his back; there was a crack and he lay still. She said:

"So this is your boyfriend."

"Carlo: meet Diana Gilbert."

He looked at us both in bewilderment. "What is this, Dawn? Why is she here?"

He obviously didn't hear me. I said, "No more questions, Carlo. Get your men in here quickly."

"But…"

"Listen to me, Carlo." I wanted to get through to him as quickly as possible. "Get your men. Get them here. Now."

Diana checked Signora Palladio's neck; then the Dominican. "Both OK: they'll live." Carlo's men came silently into the cathedral.

I said to Carlo. "Take your wife home, Carlo." He bent over and crossed himself. He motioned to Franco, who with one of his colleagues lifted her gently and left the building.

Carlo stared at me. "I still don't understand, Dawn."

"There is nothing to understand, Carlo. Go home. Look after your wife. Goodbye."

He stared at me once more, then left.

Diana said: "What do we do with this idiot?"

"Leave him. We'll collect the photos and get out of here. Somebody will find him early in the morning. It'll be their problem." We walked quickly to the rear of the Duomo until we reached the other car. One of Franco's colleagues was behind the wheel.

He got out, and recognised me. "Signorina?"

"Do you know the motor hotel near Malpensa?"

"Si."

"Then take us there, please."

Diana threw her grip on the back seat and followed it into the Merc; I sat in the front. I said to the driver, "What did Signor Palladio tell you?"

"Nothing, signorina. Just to obey your instructions."

"OK. But I need you to know that we were saving the family's reputation. There was no blasphemy committed. Understood?"

He nodded and drove on. Diana and I sat silently all the way to the airport hotel. Both with our own thoughts. Mine, of course, about Carlo: when I said 'goodbye' that was what it was; I would not see him again. How did I feel? Strangely, nothing; I was empty of feeling. Surely I must feel something after tonight's drama – and the violence. But no: perhaps delayed shock would hit me. I glanced in the rear-view mirror:

Diana was fast asleep. I looked through the window, at the blackness pricked by distant lights, then I dozed.

***

So that was the end of that affair, and also my affaire with Carlo. There was something almost biblical – Old Testament – in the fracas at the Duomo when I look back on it. When Carlo contacted me with his urgent appeal I of course reported immediately to Commander Maddox (you didn't really expect me to do otherwise, did you?) and Diana was my shadow during the whole operation. What happened next? Well, the details first. Carlo's driver took us to the airport hotel; we booked a twin room; showered, changed into 'business women's' clothes (Diana sprang on the scene in the cathedral dressed like me, a la commando); we dumped my tracksuit and trainers in a trash can; and strolled into the hotel bar without a care in the world. We turned heads in there as we sipped champagne. We had a bit of fun with the young males near us by holding hands and staring into each other's eyes.

Reception had an electronic board behind the desk detailing flight times: we booked two seats and caught the first flight to Gatwick the following day, then went our separate ways as we passed through Border Control. I was tempted to show my Customs ID, but resisted it.

So what happened to Carlo and his wife? Later that week I Googled the Italian Press. There was an AP report, saying that, due to his wife's serious illness, Signor Palladio had withdrawn his candidature for MEP. None of the photos ever saw the light of day (Diana and I had seen to that).

But what of the fuss about the paintings – the so-called lost or stolen works of art? My obsession had misled me: I made too many assumptions. In the story in the Italian papers and TV about Carlo – almost as an afterthought – it mentioned his charitable work and his presence at the Venice Biennale (remember that?). It seems he was a member of a committee set up by The Commission for Looted Art to try to trace all the 'lost' paintings that had not been uncovered since World War II; those that I had printed off from his computer at his London office. Still, I suppose it wasn't all in vain. I no longer loved Carlo, but I suppose I owed him a lot – and not just in material terms. I would call it fifty-fifty.

Oh, and one final thing. About a month later I received a statement from my bank in Switzerland: 50, 000 euros had been deposited in my account. Thanks, again, Carlo.

Finale: Operation Payback

Somewhere in Norfolk
One Year Later

I woke from the hard mattress and looked through the smeared, cobweb-covered window. I was wearing (and had slept in) a dark-blue, fleece-lined anorak and dark jeans tucked into wool socks; on my feet, hiking boots. I rubbed the four small panes with my sleeve; it left a greasy, cobwebbed stain on the new fabric. I peered through the window; across the long flat landscape there was an edge of white light, as the day slowly took shape. Even dressed in operational gear, I had woken cold, my body temperature having lowered while I was dozing. I said:

"Is there any coffee left in that flask?"

Diana Gilbert said, "If we're lucky." She had woken me after her patrol; as laid down in these circumstances, it was two hours duty, one hour off. We had been at this station since 9 p.m. (21.00 hours, if one wished to be pedantic) the previous evening, stuck in an old Dutch barn, hiding behind a stack of hay bales. It was the end of March, but still damn cold, and I thought yet again why I considered it might be interesting – or even intellectually challenging – to work for Her Majesty's Revenue and Customs. It was very quiet and still where we were positioned, but we were only too well aware of the wind sweeping across the fields and through the barn.

Diana peered through the night-sight binoculars. "Nothing; not a bloody thing."

She shared the coffee with me: thankfully, it still had some heat in it. She stopped me. "Here," she said, "try some of this in it." She took a hip flask and poured the contents into the mugs. I could smell the brandy; it seared down my throat. I said:

"Booze is against the rules. Does Maddox know?"

"Of course not, and bollocks to Maddox. I'll also have you know that I pinched some of Max's best cognac. Put it down to 'operational necessity'."

I looked through the window again: the dawn was breaking rapidly now, and it looked as though this whole stake-out was going to be a complete waste of time. It reminded me only too well of the training exercises I had gone through earlier in the year. And it also made me ask: how on earth did I find myself in this position, stuck in an old Norfolk barn, half frozen, with this crazy girl Diana?

I dropped that thought as Diana nudged me. "Look." She passed the binoculars to me. I could just make out the vehicle moving in our direction; we were stationed just off the B1155 near Syderstone, and the van – from its movement – must have been heading southwards on the B1454 (*Heading for the A148?*).

We waited. Then it changed direction. We were wrong: it was turning to the B1155; straight towards us. We gathered our gear quickly, then I made mobile contact and advised the police of our position as we moved out of the barn and scrambled to the rear of the farmhouse; we were now in shadow. A light came on in an upstairs window. We waited. The pick-up (with canvas hood) hove into view; it had English number plates; it was a dark-green Ford; so they'd got that right. But its lights were not on.

Diana and I moved out of the shadows as the two police Volvos, blue lights flashing, performed a pincer movement in the farmyard, cutting off the Ford. In panic, two men sprang from the cab and ran off. The nearest to me changed direction, but ran straight into the grip of a uniformed constable. The larger of them rushed at Diana, obviously intending to push her away or knock her over; but she seemed to go with his force, and the next I saw was him spinning to the ground and landing on his back in straw and mud.

He yelled and cursed. So: Spanish. Diana now had her boot on his wrist. I stood over him and spoke in his own language.

"Who are you? I am an officer from English Revenue and Customs and you are nicked (I've always wanted to say that). What is your name?"

"Fuck off, you English cow."

We were wasting our time. The uniformed sergeant came across. "Everything OK?"

He looked at the Spaniard, and laughed. "He looks a bit fed up!"

The sergeant and two constables marched the two men off, handcuffed. The farmer had emerged during this fracas in his dressing gown; a constable brought him across. He was middle-aged, bleary-eyed, and overweight. Diana asked, "Is there anyone else in the house?"

He nodded, "My wife," then pulled an ancient sweater over his bulging belly.

One of the constables took charge of him, cautioned him, then said, "Listen to what these two people say."

I said, "My colleague and I are officers from Revenue and Customs. We have a warrant to search these premises. Do you understand, Mr White?" He didn't reply. I said to the constable: "We've got to inspect the vehicle and outbuildings. Are you taking them both to the station?"

"That's right. But how are you going to get back?"

"Our Land Rover is parked behind that bit of woodland."

He looked over my shoulder. "I see. You mean that rust-bucket? You'll have to watch that I don't charge you under the Road Traffic Act." He handcuffed White, then handed him to his colleague who put him in one of the police cars.

"Very amusing, Mr Policeman. Please tell your Super what we are doing." He grinned and left.

Diana and I entered the house by the stone steps, which led straight into the kitchen, a long, narrow room with a stone floor. The kitchen was lit by a fluorescent tube set between two oak beams, stained by years of smoke and grease, leaving a shiny patina, the sort of muck that antique dealers drool over. There was an equally long pine table. Sitting at the table was a woman with her back to the Aga. She was younger than her husband; at least we assumed she was married to the farmer. In front of her was a brown teapot and a mug; steam rose from it; in her left hand she held a cigarette. We introduced ourselves. She didn't seem surprised.

"I've just brewed; d'you want a cup?"

We accepted.

"Are you Mrs White?"

She drew on the cigarette and blinked at us through the smoke.

"For my sins." She was incongruous in this rough setting; a handsome woman; oval face; wide-set dark eyes; generous mouth; high forehead; dark hair. Diana said:

"Do you know why we're here, Mrs White?"

She stubbed out the cigarette. "I can guess. I've been warning Harold for ages."

"So you knew that he was involved in smuggling and receiving?"

A wary look came into her dark eyes. "I didn't say that. I knew he was involved in some sort of scam – he usually is. I kept out of it. I'm his wife, cook, and occasional bedmate. Not his keeper." She pulled her robe – an expensive-looking garment in dark silk – tighter round her nightdress. Diana and I exchanged glances: we both noticed the 'occasional'. She said: "Now; do you mind if I get dressed? I suppose I've got to go with him."

"You suppose correctly, Mrs White."

Diana took all the house keys from Mrs White, labelled them, and scribbled a receipt, which she gave to the police sergeant.

We locked the house behind us and moved across the yard to the barn. It was a stout, corrugated iron building with a hefty lock attached to an iron bar set into the double doors. Diana fiddled with the bunch of keys and inserted one into the lock. It opened easily (obviously well oiled). We slid back the doors which were hung on casters. Wooden and cardboard boxes were stacked neatly, as if in a normal warehouse.

Diana said: "You'd think it was Argos."

The barn was only about a third full of the boxes, but sufficient for us to see that it was a mini-Aladdin's cave. But what was surprising was that on top of each box were trays of flowers, young, shooting bedding plants; they stretched out in a blaze of colour. Diana and I looked at each other in surprise: of course, that was the Whites' front; a plant nursery. We went for the wooden crates first, carefully stacking the trays of plants on the barn floor. Diana used a crowbar, slowly prising away the lid.

There were six of them measuring about 50cm x 50cm, but what we were looking for was underneath. Wrapped in waterproof, oilskin bundles was enough cannabis and cocaine to make White and his cohorts rich men. But we had to list all the contents of the boxes. It took us more than two hours; the boring part of our job. We were tired, hungry, and fed up.

The farm house was the CID's job. Diana used the Department cell-phone to contact the police station. She said, "We're finished here; you can send in your scene of crime officers." They weren't long in coming, but none too pleased that we had invaded their virgin territory. I briefed them and we left.

'The rust bucket' (as that cheeky big copper called it) took us to our digs. Diana drove the Land Rover (this was her home county, after all) along the B1454 past Docking and straight to Heacham, south of Hunstanton. Thankfully, we didn't have to stay there. Our 'safe house' – which we grandly called it – was a B&B run by the wife of a retired police sergeant. It was typical of the tall, narrow, three-storey, redbrick Norfolk houses that had been used as holiday escapes by working families for generations. Diana and I had the last room on the top floor, with twin beds and our own bathroom (such luxury!). We removed all our gear; I glanced at the front window of the old house. The notice said, NO VACANCIES.

Mrs Swann opened the door as soon as we stood on the step. We were enveloped by an embrace of warm air, as we squeezed down the narrow hall and dropped our bags against the umbrella stand. Mrs Swann looked us over in a motherly fashion. "Everything all right, dear?" Mrs Swann is a formidable woman; an archetype of the seaside landlady – but a kindly soul.

Diana asked: "How's Mr Swann?"

"Jack's all right, thank you. He's in his shed at the end of the garden," she replied – as if he'd be anywhere else. "Now: your beds are made up and there are clean towels, so up you go. Your lunch will be ready in half an hour." That sounded like an order.

Diana and I stripped off our working gear and stood in long johns and wool vests in the cosy (i.e. small) bedroom; nobody would wear frilly smalls where we had spent the night. At one time, I would have been too self-conscious to stand naked in front of Diana (it never bothered her) but now we hardly noticed; we were too eager to get under the shower. We stood back-to-back and let the hot soapy water run over us.

Dried and covered in baby talc, we donned clean underwear and large fluffy white robes. We grinned at each other while we brushed our hair. I said:

"You know, something Diana?"

"What's that?"

"When we first did this…"

"You mean bathing together?"

"Yes. Well, it passed through my mind that you could have a touch of the Sappho in you."

Diana was amused. "As a matter of fact, I did have fling with a college friend; but that was a long time ago."

I was intrigued. "Really? Oh. What was it like?"

"I was a virgin – it was really rather exciting. In a funny kind of way, it made me want a man."

"And how did that work out?"

"Wonderful; he was the head waiter at the place where I had a summer job. He was divorced and hadn't been close to a woman for at least two years. Just think! I was deflowered by shy, skinny individual with a degree in medieval history in the attic of a seaside hotel."

It made me wonder what a man with a history degree was doing working as a waiter in a hotel. I said: "We'd better get down before Mrs S ticks us off." But before we left our room, I phoned my father on my personal mobile – 'reporting in', as he and I termed it.

"Dawn: did the day go well? Did the forces of justice prevail?"

"Perfectly, Dad. I'll see you tomorrow."

Pulling her robe round her, Diana asked: "Do you ever think of Carlo?"

I was surprised at the question; I didn't really know what to say. But I replied,

"No: hardly ever, Diana. Strange, isn't it?"

"You went through a lot for him, Dawn. Any feelings left?"

"No," I said sharply.

Then Diana changed tack: "Your father's a real eccentric professor, isn't he? Is that right: that he's always entertaining John Hibbert?"

"He seems to have taken a shine to him," I said crossly. "Dad seems fascinated by John's profession – a closed world to an elderly scholar. I come home and he's sat in the study with Dad, drinking tea."

"Anything else?"

"He keeps bringing me flowers, and inviting me out to dinner."

"Have you accepted?"

"Once or twice," I mumbled. "He seems to be able to book a table at The Ivy at short notice."

"Well, well… You could do worse, Dawn. He's a decent bloke. Your father likes him. And I think you're just being a stubborn, pouty woman. Go for it, kid."

"Well, you've met my father. I was rather hoping Anne Holt would have had a benign influence on him by now – seems as though she might be part of the plot! Do not be deceived! He can put on an act to get his own way, just like all the elderly gents."

"You want to try living with Max – awkward old sod!"

We sat round Mrs Swann's kitchen table in front of enormous pieces of battered haddock and chips. She poured tea that looked as if it would do a good job restoring walnut furniture. Her husband, Jack, joined us from the garden, followed by Sam, an old woolly-haired dog who sniffed near our chairs then ignored us, plonking himself by the fire. He reminded me of the dog in Renoir's painting, *At the Inn of Mother Anthony*, looking out of the picture, as if to say, 'Who are you? What do you want?' To my mind, the doggiest dog that had ever appeared in a picture. Jack Swann looked us over swiftly, a frizzled-haired, broad-shouldered man wearing a check shirt.

"You two lasses all right?" Jack never enquired about our operations; but this time he asked. "Successful?"

Diana said, "It should be; the operation has been tracking for weeks. But now we think we've got the evidence and the culprits." She turned to Mrs Swann, "We have to report to Hunstanton later; we don't know how long we will be. Is it OK if we have the room tonight, Mrs Swann?"

"Of course, I'll let you have the key."

We returned to our bedroom and I set the alarm for 4 p.m. – two hours' sleep for us both, before we sat in on the police questioning of the two Spaniards. I fell asleep immediately, dreaming of Carlo; I was trying to find him in the dream, chasing all over Milan: I suppose that was a Freudian guilt trip after what happened to his wife.

Fifteen minutes after waking, we were dressed (business-like dark trouser suits over white silk shirts); we looked like pushy young lawyers from a classy City firm.

Diana drove the 'rust bucket' to Hunstanton and parked in Lynn Road at the Police station. As we got out of the car I could feel the stiff breeze off the sea. I was wearing a thick scarf and anorak over the trouser suit, but I still felt cold. I said to Diana, "Is it always as cold as this in the spring here?"

Diana grinned. "You should try it in January: it blows straight from the Russian steppes. It's as cold as a witch's tit."

"What a charming old-fashioned turn of phrase you use."

As we walked in, a young, large-eyed woman constable eyed us over, then examined our ID, which identified us as officers of the HM Revenue & Customs: our photos behind plastic with stamps and signatures (which nearly obliterated our face); set in a black leather wallet, with the opposite side stamped in gold with the Crown over a portcullis. The constable said:

"Is that your Land Rover parked there?"

"Yes."

"Then I'll need its number, please. It's a bit of a wreck, isn't it? Can't you do better than that? I should complain if I were you."

"You try telling our boss." She grinned and gave us directions to the superintendent's office; and – surprise, surprise – John Hibbert was waiting for us. He looked at us warily, then turned to an older man, saying, "These ladies are from Revenue and Customs, sir."

"So these are the deadly duo, are they?" he grinned and held out his hand. "I'm Superintendent Baxter." He was a thin man of medium height, very neatly dressed; white shirt with club tie; a half inch of white cuff peeked from the jacket sleeve; highly polished black shoes.

Diana asked, "What's the situation, Mr Baxter?"

Baxter was leaning against the front of his desk; now he stood and strolled round the office. "Well, first of all Mr and Mrs White have been transferred to Norwich, as they seem to be the principals in this case." (*Norwich? Great Yarmouth was Norfolk Constabulary's HQ*). He stopped walking, then said, "The two Spanish chaps are in different cells, awaiting your initial interviews. All we know is that they work as waiters in the Promenade Hotel in Lynn, and will speak only in Spanish. Try to get as much info as possible, ladies – the usual: how long they've been in the country, etc.; how they met White. You know the drill." He turned at looked at Inspector Hibbert. "And no doubt your colleague will be taping all this?"

I said: "You don't want much! I have to remind you, Superintendent, that there is a division of labour in this case: Our duty is to apprehend the alleged culprits; establish their identity; and record the seized cargo and report this to our HQ in London. Then it is up to you or Norwich Division to take it from there. How long do you think this will take?"

He thrust his hands in his trouser pockets, threw back his head, thought for a moment, then said, "In my experience, quite a long time! Never mind, we'll keep you supplied with cartons of tea." He smiled in an avuncular manner at us. He said, "We'll keep you fairly isolated: we don't want my constables distracted by two pretty women, do we, Inspector Hibbert?" He nodded at us. "I think it would be in your best interests if you did that."

John Hibbert raised his eyes to heaven and did not reply. And I thought, *If anybody ever tells you it is in 'your own interests' it means exactly the opposite; you are going to be ditched – and the only person who benefits is the person who said it in the first place.*

Diana said: "How very kind, Mr Baxter. Just so we're agreed that we don't have to give evidence in Court. We are just translators. And may we point out that the most important info will come from the Whites. Did you know that he claimed to be a nurseryman? There are boxes of plants all over the place. It didn't do my hay fever any good!"

So we were stuck in stuffy interview rooms trying to get some kind of information from the two young, macho Spaniards, who obviously didn't like being cross-examined by women, accompanied by two constables, who seemed more bored than distracted. And of course DI John Hibbert. It went something like this:

"*Este es u paseporte? Su nombre es Migue/Barras?*" (It was obvious that it was his passport; it was in front of him with his name and photo.)

He just shrugged – a stupid question from the English girl.

"*Se le cobrara con el transporte de una clase de medicamentos. Me entiendes?*"

(Neither did the threat that he and his fellow smuggler would go to prison for a long time for transporting narcotics worry him.)

His arrogance was getting on my nerves. I said to John Hibbert, "We are wasting our time. I'm going to ask Mr Baxter to charge him with the murder; let's see how these two homosexuals cope with homicide, eh?" At that the Spaniard exploded into English.

"Murder! What is this murder? I kill no one! And you call me some kinda queer?"

Then he realised what he had done – then cursed me in Spanish. We had achieved our objective. Hibbert taped the remainder of his 'confession'; naturally, he blamed his companion for dragging him into the operation. Diana used the same ploy; though she had an easier job, for Jose (that what he called himself; he wasn't carrying his passport) was the one Diana clobbered at the farm.

Even so, it was late by the time we had collated the details, and we didn't get back to Mrs Swann's place until after nine that evening; who – bless her – supplied us with bowls of hot vegetable soup and fresh rolls, then vanished into her sitting room to watch TV. We opened the bottle of wine purchased from the mini-market from round the corner. Jack was sat in the kitchen-diner reading a copy of *Amateur Gardener* with the dog Sam at his feet hogging the fire.

He had set the table and put bowls of soup in front of us as soon as we sat. I said, "It almost makes it worthwhile at the end of the day to have this put in front of us, Mr Swann."

Jack frowned. "I'm sure, but it makes me wonder at times whether you lasses put yourselves into unnecessary danger."

"Oh, it's not that…"

He put up a hand as if directing traffic. "I was a copper for thirty years; you may think this is a quiet old town, but we've had some nasty characters land up here. Norfolk is a very open coast. Have you ever thought why they stationed you here? We're bang on the North Sea facing northern Europe: Holland, Scandinavia with their lax laws on narcotics – bloody fools. Sorry, girls…"

Diana said, "I'm a Norfolk girl; I know what you mean. What you say is right. But we both feel that this house is the safest place in England. Will you join us in a glass of wine?"

The following morning we left our 'safe haven' just after eight (and no doubt our room would be occupied by another couple of law officers). As we walked to where we left the 'rust bucket' I saw Jack Swann approach us; he had Sam on a lead, who loped obediently by his master's side. He eyed us, as did the dog, who immediately sat on my shoe and leaned against my leg, sighing.

"You ladies off, then? Everything tied up and written in triplicate?" He grinned after saying that. Whether he was amused by his dog or all the paperwork, I couldn't say.

I said: "Clear off, Sam, and lean on your breakfast."

"Don't remind us, Jack," said Diana. "First stop, Great Yarmouth. Can you tell me, please, Sergeant Swann, why Norfolk Constabulary decided to have its HQ in a dump like Yarmouth?"

Mr Swann looked shocked. "You mustn't say that about Yarmouth! Mrs Swann comes from there!"

"Oops."

It was a helluva long drive to Great Yarmouth; but there was nothing for it but to take the Land Rover down the A149, skirting King's Lynn (Diana disliked going near her home town) then from Norwich to Yarmouth just in time for the afternoon meeting at the police HQ. We stopped for a non-alcoholic lunch at a pub in Blofield.

There was a sergeant guarding the desk at the police station and studied our ID with some surprise – if not suspicion. "You'll be for Chief Inspector Crawley's conference, then?"

The conference room was on the first floor with a view of the rear of some old buildings (no distractions with views over the grey sea). There was a mixture of uniformed and plain-clothes officers. We sat at the rear like obedient pupils. There were two middle-aged men in dark suits sat behind a table facing us; a chart was hung on a large flip board behind them. One of them stood; he said:

"Right; I think everybody's here, from both Yarmouth and Norwich. You know me – DCI Crawley. We're also joined by DI Hibbert from Special Branch liaison," (Hibbert stood and nodded), "and the meeting is also adorned by two ladies from Customs." He smiled in our direction. Several faces looked over their shoulders. Diana grinned and waved; I blushed. Crawley continued:

"You also know that this is another chapter in Operation Payback. Last night, four arrests were made at a small-holding near Syderstone – the owner and his wife, a Gilbert and Hilda

White, and two Spaniards. All were charged with transporting or dealing in class A narcotics. Mr and Mrs White are now being questioned by detectives from Bethel Street CID in Norwich. The Spaniards have been transferred to London." (That was news to us-and a relief. I detest these macho Spanish males.)

Crawley looked across the room. He said: "DS Harrison led the SOCO team." A fair-haired woman in her thirties stood and gave the meeting a run-down.

"You'll get details later from my lads. The situation is given on the map refs. We entered the buildings almost immediately after the Customs officers were on site with the narcotics. The farmhouse was clean of any suspicious items; no drugs. No cannabis plants in the house; the only things growing were trays of young plants. Mrs White was obviously an efficient housekeeper. The Whites seemed to have separate bedrooms: all the cupboards and chests of drawers were searched. Nothing – unless you count all the designer clothes in Mrs White's extensive wardrobe, plus shoes and handbags to die for!"

Crawley interjected. "You weren't tempted to overturn the forces of law and order and help yourself, Jane?"

"Not my size, boss." Which lightened the atmosphere.

Somebody asked, "Who's guarding the premises now, sergeant?"

Jane Harrison said, "Two constables are on duty. When my team have finished, the place will be sealed."

Crawley said: "We are also conducting a house-to-house in nearby villages; first, to find if the Whites have any relatives, and second to see if we are lucky enough to have nosy neighbours."

The DCI called a halt to the meeting, and made the usual demand for reports to be on his desk ASAP. As we were leaving, Crawley beckoned in our direction, so we followed him and John Hibbert into his office. We sat in front of his desk. He said,

"Just so we're up to speed. You'll be returning to London and reporting to Commander Maddox?" Hibbert said:

"Yes, sir. We are still working on the point where the drugs entered the UK; you'll hear from Mr Maddox in due course. And thank you for your cooperation."

Crawley smiled grimly. He said: "Well, we both know that is far from the end of this business – there's a terrorist connection somewhere along the line, isn't there?"

We shook hands all round and followed John Hibbert to the police car park; the dark-blue Audi was parked next to the rust bucket. That would be left here until anyone else from London was posted here. I hope it wouldn't be us. John always seemed to 'looking after' us; and being a snooty bitch at times, the fact that he – or Maddox – thought that we needed a chaperone got up my nose. He hadn't seen Diana in action!

And I know what would happen in London. He would drop Diana home, then take me to Maida Vale; I would have to feed him and my father, who had become as thick as thieves. Sitting at the dinner table with those two is to eat alone. Just because I had fallen for John Hibbert and he me (surprise, surprise, eh?) did not mean that I liked him very much, and it didn't mean he could make himself at home here whenever he liked. One thing I would not allow: John Hibbert staying overnight.

If our feelings were that strong on occasion, he could book a hotel room. As long as it wasn't the Quest-Ritson.